73

BF

'Hannah...'

Dio, she was beautiful. Complex, mysterious and enigmatic, she excited him more than any other woman had ever done. He allowed the fingers of one hand to trace the line of freckles on her face. He heard the cadence of her breathing change and her lashes drifted shut, only to snap open again when he brushed the pad of his thumb across her lips.

'Nic?' she whispered.

His thumb under her chin, he bent his head with infinite care and touched his mouth to hers. He had longed for this. Sinking his fingers into the hair at her nape, he slowly deepened the kiss, coaxing her through her hesitancy and into willing participation, groaning at the tentative exploration as her own tongue glided with his. She tasted exquisite, fresh and pure, and he knew right away that he would never tire of kissing her, that he wanted so much more...

'Stay,' he urged softly.

Margaret McDonagh says of herself: 'I began losing myself in the magical world of books from a very young age, and I always knew that I had to write, pursuing the dream for over twenty years, often with cussed stubbornness in the face of rejection letters! Despite having numerous romance novellas, short stories and serials published, the news that my first "proper book" had been accepted by Harlequin Mills & Boon for their Medical Romance™ line brought indescribable joy! Having a passion for learning makes researching an involving pleasure, and I love developing new characters, getting to know them, setting them challenges to overcome. The hardest part is saying goodbye to them, because they become so real to me. And I always fall in love with my heroes! Writing and reading books, keeping in touch with friends, watching sport and meeting the demands of my four-legged companions keeps me well occupied. I hope you enjoy reading this book as much as I loved writing it.'

You can contact Margaret at
http://margaretmcdonagh.bravehost.com

**THE ITALIAN DOCTOR'S BRIDE
is Margaret's emotional,
heart-rending debut
novel for Mills & Boon®
Medical Romance™!**

THE
ITALIAN DOCTOR'S
BRIDE

BY
MARGARET McDONAGH

First published in Great Britain 2006
Large Print edition 2007
Harlequin Mills & Boon Limited,
Eton House, 18-24 Paradise Road,
Richmond, Surrey TW9 1SR

© Margaret McDonagh 2006

ISBN-13: 978 0 263 19538 5
ISBN-10:   0 263 19538 4

Set in Times Roman 15½ on 18½ pt.
17-0407-58045

Printed and bound in Great Britain
by Antony Rowe Ltd, Chippenham, Wiltshire

MEDITERRANEAN DOCTORS

*Let these exotic doctors
sweep you off your feet...*

*Be tantalised by their smouldering
good-looks, romanced by their fiery passion,
and warmed by the emotional power of
these strong and caring men...*

MEDITERRANEAN DOCTORS
Passionate about life, love and medicine.

With special thanks...

To: John Morton, Mr Lamont and
Professor Hannay for helping
with my research.

To: Christina Jones, Sue Haasler,
Liz Young, Kate Hardy, Hilary Johnson,
Wendy Wootton, Victoria Connelly,
Lorraine, Anne & Richard, Hsin-Yi, Gwen,
Gill and Heather for their friendship
and for believing in me.

And to Joanne and all at HM&B
for making a dream come true.

CHAPTER ONE

'SOMETHING *has* to be done.'

Dr Hannah Frost did not do panic, but the chaotic Monday morning surgery pushed her as close to it as she ever hoped to come. Being one doctor down meant that her staff were harassed and overworked. More importantly, from a safety point of view, she could not continue to give her best to her patients under such exhausting circumstances. She had to find an answer to their current predicament…and soon.

For now it was a question of maintaining focus and dealing with the heavy workload. The waiting room was already filling with patients but the problem of a replacement locum nagged at her throughout the morning until her consultations, overrunning as usual, drew to an end nearly three hours later.

'You're a grand lassie, Dr Frost.' Old Mr Ferguson balanced unsteadily, both walking sticks clasped in one gnarled hand as he reached out with the other to pat her arm. 'It was a lucky day for us all when you chose to come back to Lochanrig to be our doctor.'

'Thank you. This is my home and I'm happy to be here.' Hannah smiled, touched by her elderly patient's words.

She could never imagine living and working anywhere else. The responsibility of taking over the running of the practice from her father weighed heavily upon her because she cared so much, both for her patients and the family tradition. These were her people. The rugged beauty of this part of south-west Scotland was her home. She felt safe here. Her challenges were professional, not personal. Hannah suppressed an inner shiver. She didn't do personal. Not any more.

Conscious of Mr Ferguson's frailty, and aware of his fierce independence, she pushed her thoughts away and moved slowly by his side as he shuffled from her consulting room towards the reception area where Jim Henderson, the local taxi driver, was waiting.

'All ready now?' Jim placed a protective hand under Mr Ferguson's arm. 'Don't you worry, Doc, I'll make sure he arrives home safely.'

'Thanks, Jim. I'll see you next week, Mr Ferguson, but ring any time if you need me.'

'Aye, lass, thank you.'

Hannah held the door open for them, then turned to survey the empty waiting room with weary satisfaction before smiling ruefully at Kirsty Gordon, her practice manager and chief receptionist.

'I know, I'm running hideously late…again.'

Kirsty, in her early fifties, small in stature if not in personality and famous for speaking her mind, gave a wry grimace. 'I thought Mr Ferguson was here for the day.'

'He's lonely since his wife died two months ago. He needs a bit of time at the moment.'

'Poor man,' Kirsty allowed, her dark brows puckering in a frown. 'But it's not surprising you're exhausted the way you devote so much of yourself to everyone, Hannah. You're taking on too much alone.'

'Which is why we're trying so hard to find a new locum.'

'Let's hope they'll be better than the last one.'

Kirsty's tone was derisive and Hannah had a sneaking suspicion that an 'I told you so' lurked unspoken, hovering between them. Her practice manager had advised against Dr Lane's appointment and Hannah silently admitted that she had made a mistake. To say the young locum had been unsatisfactory was an understatement. Now they were in this mess.

'It's not easy, attracting people to an over-stretched, rural Scottish practice at the best of times,' she reflected, setting the tray of patient notes from morning surgery on the counter, ready for filing. 'But with there being such a shortage of doctors willing to work in general practice at the moment, it's proving harder than usual.'

'Maybe I have some good news for you, then!'

Hannah's green eyes widened at Kirsty's grin. 'You've heard from the agency?'

'About an hour ago.'

'And?'

'Your plan to look further afield may have paid off. They think they've found our perfect doctor. An Italian—Nicola someone—who is interested in a six-month contract and who speaks fluent English, has excellent references and an impressive CV. The agency are faxing the information through to me.'

'Fantastic!' Hannah sighed with relief, grateful for Kirsty's efficiency. 'If all the paper work is in order, we can have a chat on the phone, and the sooner she can start the better.'

'Why don't you leave it all to me? I'll do the ground

work and you can check over the information and make a decision. That would save you some time.'

'Are you sure, Kirsty? It isn't as if you have nothing to do yourself.'

'It will be fine. According to the agency, Nicola is on holiday this week so may not be easy to reach. I'll see to everything, Hannah, don't worry.'

Thankful that the locum problem might soon be resolved, she felt confident about handing the initial responsibility over to her manager. 'Thanks, Kirsty, that would be a big help. Any queries, let me know. Right,' she added, checking her watch and stifling a groan, 'I'd better be away for the house calls if I'm ever to start afternoon surgery on time.'

'Speaking of house calls, Mary McFee rang. She sounded shaky and her chest was rough.'

'OK.' Hannah frowned, concerned for the elderly lady who insisted on living alone in her isolated home. 'I'm heading out that way to see Joe MacLean, aren't I? I'll pop in and check on Mary at the same time.'

'As if you aren't busy enough,' Kirsty tutted with disapproval. 'Hopefully we'll have some help around here soon.'

Gathering the notes for the patients she had to visit, Hannah left the surgery, heartily seconding Kirsty's final statement.

* * *

Dr Nicola di Angelis's CV was certainly impressive, Hannah acknowledged later, grabbing a hasty late lunch at her desk and looking over the papers Kirsty had prepared for her. Two years younger than her own age of thirty-three, the Italian had experience in trauma and general practice, having worked in Italy, Canada and the UK. The latter included six months in a busy London A and E department eighteen months ago, followed by three months' GP work in Sussex. The letters of recommendation were glowing.

'I thought you might want to speak with the department head at the hospital in Milan where Nicola last worked,' Kirsty suggested, setting a cup of coffee down on Hannah's desk. 'I checked out the UK references and everything is fine.'

Hannah smiled, sipping the welcome drink. 'Thanks, Kirsty. Yes, I'll ring now. Everything looks to be in order. You feel happy about the appointment?'

'Indeed. From all I have heard, Nicola di Angelis is professionally respected and personally admired.'

Hannah glanced up, puzzled by the inflection in the older woman's voice. 'Let's hope she is.'

'I'll leave you to it.' Kirsty rose to her feet. 'If this last reference is good, you'll offer Nicola the job?'

'Definitely. Let's just hope she is willing to come here.'

'Good, I'm sure it's the best thing. Say if I can do anything else.'

'I appreciate all your help, Kirsty.'

After her practice manager had gone, Hannah reached for the phone and dialled the number of the Milan hospital, hoping this verbal reference would be as encouraging as the written ones.

'*Buongiorno. Pronto Soccorso,*' an efficient-sounding man announced when Hannah was connected to Accident and Emergency.

'Hello, do you speak English?' she enquired.

'*Sì.* I help you, yes?'

'Thank you. My name is Dr Hannah Frost and I'm calling from Scotland. May I speak with Francesca Simone about a reference?'

'A moment please.'

As Hannah waited, she glanced through the paperwork on Nicola di Angelis, reviewing the impressive CV once more.

'Dr Frost? I am Francesca Simone,' a voice introduced in halting English. 'What help can I be for you?'

Hannah exchanged pleasantries and explained the reason for her call. 'I understand Dr Nicola di

Angelis worked for you in Trauma. Are you able to provide a reference?'

'But, yes. Trauma and general clinics. A wonderful doctor. We were sorry to say goodbye. The patients, they love Dr di Angelis. The staff also.'

The woman gave a throaty chuckle, but before Hannah could question her further, she heard an alarm sounding in the background.

'*Scusi*, Dr Frost. I am needed. An emergency.'

'Of course. Thank you, you've been very helpful.'

'*Prego*. Dr di Angelis will not disappoint you.'

Hanging up, Hannah had to admit that, given all the evidence, it looked as if Nicola di Angelis might indeed be their perfect doctor. Glancing at her watch with a grimace, she decided there was just time to email the Italian before surgery began. She outlined the job offer, explained a little about the practice and clicked on 'Send'. Hopefully it would not be too long before a reply came back. Satisfied, Hannah updated Kirsty on progress, then turned her attention to the full patient list she had for the afternoon.

Despite a disturbed night, during which she had been called out twice, Hannah was at her desk early the next morning. With luck she would have nearly an hour before morning surgery to tackle the mountain of paperwork that increasingly plagued a GP's life. Switching on her computer, she sipped her first coffee of the day and, stifling a yawn, logged on, to find several emails waiting in her inbox.

Aside from some unwanted adverts and offers from medical supply and drug companies, she discovered a personal message from her friend Lauren, a doctor with whom she had trained and who was now working in paediatrics at a hospital in Edinburgh. But it was another message that claimed her attention. A reply from Nicola di Angelis.

Dear Dr Frost,

Thank you for your email and your offer of a contract to work alongside you in your practice for six months. The information you provided was most interesting to me. I would be happy to accept the position and will be in touch so we can make further arrangements.

I am presently in France, nearing the end of a short holiday. Depending on your needs, I would be free to start work any time from next week onwards. I have all the necessary paperwork and permits to allow this.

Kind regards,

Nicola di Angelis

Relief flooded through her as she read the message a second time. Kirsty would be delighted, as would all the practice staff who, together, worked so hard, serving their rural community. Her promise to tackle the outstanding paperwork forgotten, Hannah composed a reply straight away.

Dear Nicola,

Thank you for your swift reply and acceptance of the position. All of us here are glad that you will be joining us. We would be grateful if you could begin work as soon as possible. Next week would suit us perfectly, unless you need more time.

Please contact me or my practice manager, Kirsty Gordon, to confirm the details and ask if there is any further information you require.

Best wishes,

Hannah Frost

Her task completed, Hannah left her consulting room and, hearing chatter coming from the staffroom, went to pass on the news.

'Dr di Angelis has accepted the locum contract.'

'Excellent!' Kirsty grinned. 'Any start date given?'

'Maybe as early as next week. I've asked her to

contact you, Kirsty, if I'm unavailable. I've sent you copies of the emails.'

Kirsty nodded. 'No problem.'

'This is wonderful,' Morag, the efficient and maternal practice nurse, agreed. 'We've all been worried about you, Hannah. You've taken the brunt of everything since Dr Lane departed.'

Shona, one of the district nurses, snorted in derision. 'Not that Dr Lane did much when she was here. I hope this new one is more dedicated to our patients.'

A series of locums had come their way since her father's untimely death three years previously had left her in sole charge of the practice. Some had been good, some not so good, but none had been persuaded to stay in the locality for very long. The swift departure of Dr Lane barely two weeks into a six-month contract had been a severe blow and had plunged the whole practice into chaos.

'Let's hope Nicola di Angelis proves as perfect as her qualifications and references suggest,' she murmured now.

A speculative gleam brightened Kirsty's eyes. 'You may even discover a life outside the surgery, Hannah.'

'I'm a doctor, I don't have a social life.' And she didn't want one, she added silently. Disconcerted, Hannah turned her attention to the district nurse on duty. 'Shona, I was out at Mary McFee's yesterday and her chest is sounding grim again. She's adamant she won't be moved, but her place is terribly damp. The dry, warm summer seems to have made little difference and I'm worried about her being there for another winter.'

Brown eyes thoughtful, Shona nodded. 'I'll talk to Debbie and we'll keep a check on her.'

'Thanks.' Hannah was relieved. She knew how dedicated and reliable the two district nurses were. 'Right, I expect there's a full list again this morning so I had better press on. Send the first one through when you're ready, Kirsty.'

She had been right—it *was* another busy surgery. Amongst other things her case load included a suspected stomach ulcer, a woman with unexplained pelvic pain, a few colds and coughs, a ten-year-old with probable appendicitis, who had to be despatched to hospital, a toddler with eczema, confirmation of a pregnancy for a young couple delighted to be expecting their first baby and, lastly, Allan Pollock, who ran the local garage.

'What can I do for you today, Allan?' she greeted him, trying to hide her weariness as the stocky, middle-aged man sat down at her desk.

'It's my knee,' he explained. 'I've been taking the

paracetamol or ibuprofen when I had a painful spell, like you said last time, but it's more swollen now and is annoying me most of the time.'

Hannah nodded sympathetically and rose to her feet. 'OK, let's have you sitting on the table so I can have a look at you. Can you roll your trouser legs up, please—and don't be telling me you only washed one knee!'

'As if I'd kid you, Doc,' he protested with mock innocence, blue eyes twinkling.

'Mmm!' Smiling, Hannah began her examination, gently assessing Allan's joint. 'The left knee is very inflamed. Do you find the damp, cool weather affects it at all?'

He nodded in agreement. 'It is worse then. And when I've been sitting a while, it's hard to get moving again.'

'It's important to keep up some gentle exercise,' Hannah encouraged, probing the joint carefully. 'I'll prescribe you some non-steroidal anti-inflammatory tablets, which should help with the swelling and the discomfort. I'd also like you to see Murray McGiven, the physiotherapist, as he should be able to give you a programme to help maintain movement. The next step is to arrange an X-ray so we can see what's going on, then we can adjust your medication as necessary.'

'You think it's arthritis?'

As Allan lowered his trouser legs and slipped down from the table, Hannah returned to her desk, aware of his concern. 'With your history, it is most likely. I'll refer you for the X-ray and you'll get an appointment through the post,' she told him, turning for a moment to tap out a prescription for the NSAIDS, waiting as the printer delivered it before signing her name. 'You should be fine with these, Allan, but if you have any side-effects or stomach pains, let me know and we'll change you to something else.'

'Thanks, Doc.' He folded the prescription and put it in his pocket. 'Kirsty was telling me you might have a new locum starting soon?'

'Yes, hopefully.'

'Anything I can do to help?'

Hannah smiled. 'I was going to come and see you. I'll need to sort out a vehicle for her—a four-by-four like mine to cope with the terrain and whatever the winter weather throws at us.'

'Not like that sporty piece the last doctor arrived in!' he joked.

'Indeed.'

'You leave it with me, Doc, I'll see you right. You know Dorothy and I will never forget what you did for our Barrie.'

Hannah remembered two summers ago when the boy, then eight, had suffered bee stings. The allergic reaction had been frightening and she had been worried at the outcome of his anaphylaxis. It had needed several doses of adrenalin, followed by anti-histamine and intravenous hydrocortisone, before things had been brought under control and Barrie had been stabilised for transfer to hospital.

'How's he doing?'

'He's grand, Doc.' Allan beamed. 'Always up to mischief.'

'Takes after his father, does he?'

Allan laughed and stood up. 'I'll let you know about the vehicle, Doc.'

'Thank you. And no special favours. You have a living to make for your family. Promise me.'

'I'll take care of it, Doc,' was as far as he would go.

At the end of another frantically busy day, Hannah felt out on her feet. Thank goodness the rota system with the next nearest practices meant she did not have to be on call that night. Munching an apple, she wandered round the house, her memories flooding back as she recalled her childhood in this rambling old building, her parents working all hours, caring for their widespread community. Unlike some other medical facilities, they had survived changes, closures and financial cuts, and the opportunity to build the modern new surgery a decade ago had been a real bonus.

Hannah had gladly returned to work in Lochanrig. It had suited her just fine, being professionally challenging and personally safe. But losing both her parents so soon had been devastating. First her mother in a hit-and-run accident. Then, swamped with grief and working too hard, her father had driven himself to an early grave a year later. Literally. She shivered, wrapping her arms around herself, recalling that terrible day. When the call had come in for her to attend the accident on the mountain road, she had set out, not knowing the victim was her own father, that he had suffered a heart attack at the wheel and crashed, that it had already been too late to save him.

Battling her own grief, Hannah had summoned a strength she had not known she possessed to keep the practice running. A quiet determination not to fail her patients, or her family tradition, had kept her going. The one major headache had been keeping another doctor. Maybe this time it would be different.

'ETA on the air ambulance is ten minutes.'

'Thanks.' Hannah nodded towards the police constable who had slithered down the slope to deliver the information. She shook her head, looking at the tangled wreckage of the vehicle, which had run off the hill road and crashed in a gully. 'Let's hope we have this boy out of the car by then.'

'They never learn, do they? A night out in the city, too much to drink and they think they are invincible.'

Hannah nodded again. Being called out in the early hours of Sunday morning in her role as BASICS emergency doctor on call had been the last thing she had needed after an unusually hectic week. A week during which Kirsty had talked with Dr di Angelis on the telephone. Hannah would rather have spoken to the new locum herself but she had been out on house visits when the call had come in. Kirsty had been taken with their new doctor and foresaw no problems. Given the predicament the practice was in, Hannah had been content to delegate responsibility to her knowledgeable manager.

Dragging her thoughts back to the current situation, Hannah addressed the young policeman. 'At least we got the other two out quickly and away to hospital.'

'Were they badly injured?' he asked, watching as the firefighters fought to cut the driver free.

'A few broken bones, nothing that won't heal. It's this one I'm worried about.'

'Foolish bloke wasn't wearing a seat belt, I hear,' the constable remarked.

'That's right. He has a very nasty head injury.'

'Should—? I mean, don't you need to be with him?'

Hannah glanced at the young policeman and saw alarm mixed with curiosity in his eyes. 'I've done what I can to stabilise him and have fitted a neck brace. One of the paramedics is in the car, keeping his head still while they cut him out. No room for all of us while the fire crew are working.'

'I see. Thanks, Doc. I've not been to many of these.'

'They are never pleasant, I'm afraid.'

The sound of the helicopter alerted them to the arrival of the specialist medical team. Hovering for several moments, searching for a safe place to land, the yellow aircraft finally dropped out of sight round a bend in the road above them, just as the early October dawn was breaking over the eastern hills.

Hannah breathed a sigh of relief when she recognised the experienced Dr Stewart scrambling down the gully towards her, a paramedic behind him.

'Morning, Archie,' she greeted with a brief smile. 'Sorry to bring you out.'

'What have we got, Hannah?'

'Male driver, early twenties. Serious head trauma. He's been unconscious since I arrived. No seat belt worn. Suspected high alcohol intake. I've stabilised him as best I can. His airway has been secured, he's having oxygen and I fitted a neck brace. There's a paramedic with him, monitoring his head while he's being cut out. There is not much outward blood loss but some seepage of fluid and blood from the nose and ears, which may mean he has a basal skull fracture. He also has facial fractures. We've put a line in and are giving saline and analgesia. Pupils are even but slow to react. Glasgow coma scale about 5 or 6. No sign of thoracic or abdominal injury but he's trapped by his lower legs—there will likely be trauma there when he's free and can be assessed,' she summed up, adding details of pulse and blood pressure.

'Good work,' Archie Stewart praised. 'We'll get a muscle blockade into him before he's moved. How long until they have him out of there?'

'Only a few more moments, I hope. It's been a struggle.'

His experienced blue gaze scanned the tangled wreckage. 'I can see that. Anyone else hurt?'

'Two other young males. Broken bones and cuts only. They've gone to hospital by road ambulance.'

'And how are things with you? Heard you were looking for a locum again.'

Hannah raised an eyebrow. 'Word certainly gets around. We have a new doctor due this coming week.'

'There's always a place for you in trauma if you get fed up with the hassles of general practice.'

Hannah shook her head. 'Thanks, but I enjoy what I do.'

A flurry of activity near the wreck and a call from a firefighter told them the casualty was ready to be moved and curtailed further conversation. Hannah followed as Archie scrambled to the wreckage to assess what was now his patient and supervise the extraction. It took several minutes more before he was happy, then agonising moments as the patient was carefully transferred, his head and neck immobilised with tapes and sandbags, and he was safely secured for the dangerous trip ahead.

'Right, we're away to Glasgow,' Archie announced, as they finally scrambled out of the gully and reached the road. 'Good job, Hannah.'

'Thanks.'

She lingered with the rescue workers as the group bearing the young man disappeared round the bend in the road. They heard the helicopter start up and after a few moments it lifted above the stone outcrop and into the sky, before heading north.

'Do you think the guy will make it?' The fire

officer in charge grimaced as his team gathered up their equipment.

'Hard to tell. He's very poorly. But you've all done a terrific job as usual, and given him the best chance,' Hannah smiled, her praise including the road paramedics and the young policeman who also lingered nearby. 'Thanks for your help.'

The firefighters grinned. 'You too, Doc.'

'Fancy a coffee back at base?' one of the paramedics asked.

Hannah craved lashings of strong, hot coffee, but at home. Alone. 'Thanks, but I'd best get back to Lochanrig. I need a clean-up and some breakfast.'

It was a relief to turn in between the old stone pillars that marked the entrance to the house half an hour later, but as she headed up the gravel drive, she groaned at the sight of a motorbike parked to one side.

'Oh, no. What now?'

Still wearing the grubby coveralls and BASICS jacket she had donned to work at the crash site, she climbed out of her car and looked around for the owner of the motorbike. Although a helmet was propped on the seat and a bag rested on the ground, no one was in sight. Sighing, she went round to the boot and took out her medical case. Feeling tired and dishevelled after hours of crawling around the twisted wreckage of the car, she walked towards the house. As she fumbled for her key, she heard footsteps in the gravel behind her. Heart sinking, she turned round, hoping there was not some other emergency requiring her attention.

Her eyes widened as she saw a man approaching. His gait loose-limbed, he exuded an easy confidence and self-assurance. She felt distinctly on edge. As he came closer, she could see he was incredibly good-looking in a rugged and dangerous kind of way, his raven-black hair short but thick, his dark eyes watchful as his disturbing gaze raked over her. Tense, Hannah instinctively stepped back towards the door, tamping down a rush of deep-seated anxiety.

Her breath lodging in her throat, Hannah faced the dark stranger. An inch or so under six feet, he cut an imposing figure, athletically built and wearing faded, figure-hugging jeans and a battered dark brown leather jacket. His face was classically sculpted, with the merest hint of a cleft in his determined chin. Smouldering dark eyes watched her intently.

'What do you want?' she challenged, the uncharacteristic snap in her voice evidence of the reawakening of her inner fears at this unexpected and unwanted confrontation.

His sensuous mouth curved at her feisty reaction. 'Dr Frost?'

Hannah faced him warily, flicking back strands of wayward chestnut hair which had escaped her hurried braid. 'You need medical attention?' she queried doubtfully, seldom having seen anyone in better health.

'No!' He unleashed a killer smile, his voice huskily accented as he continued, 'It is good to meet you at last, Hannah. I am Dr Nicola di Angelis.'

CHAPTER TWO

DEAR God, no! Hannah stared at him in horrified disbelief, uncharacteristic panic forming a heavy knot in her stomach. 'But you can't be.'

'There is a problem?'

'You're supposed to be a woman.'

He raised one dark eyebrow, quizzical amusement glittering in his eyes at her accusatory tone. 'I can assure you, Hannah, I am very much a man.'

'Look,' she began, flustered by the huskiness of his accented voice, disturbed by his presence and his blatant masculinity, 'there's obviously been some mistake.'

'It is necessary to discuss this in the driveway?'

Hannah didn't want to discuss it at all. She just wanted him to get on his bike and go back where he had come from. How could she have been so stupid? Had Kirsty deliberately allowed her to believe their new locum was a woman? The practice manager had spoken to him, for goodness' sake, and hadn't corrected her when she had referred to Nicola as 'she'. But what could she have done if she had realised? She pressed her hand to her temple. She had just never considered this possibility. The fact that he was so...so *male* made it worse.

'I do not understand. Why is this such a difficulty?' he probed, clearly perplexed by her reaction. 'You desperately need a doctor, do you not?'

'Yes, but—'

'But?'

'Nicola is a girl's name,' Hannah rallied, her insides churning at the disaster unfolding before her. 'You must have realised I would think that.'

His good humour undaunted by her coldness, he smiled. 'In Italy this is not so. And it never occurred to me that gender was an issue. You gave no indication of only requiring a woman doctor and Kirsty made no such comment when I telephoned and we discussed me working here. But, please, Hannah, call me Nic if it makes you feel better.'

It didn't make her feel better at all. Not one jot. Dear God, she needed to think, but he was right, this wasn't the place. How could she go on with this as if nothing had happened? How could she cope with him living in her house? It just wouldn't work. And just wait until she saw Kirsty!

'A doctor is wanted. I am here. Please, can we carry on now we have this misunderstanding out of the way? I have rushed to get here, knowing you needed me. I am tired and I have had a long journey. We can go inside, yes?'

'Yes. No. I mean…'

Why did he have to be so reasonable, so right? Why did she have to start behaving like some flustered teenager rather than the mature and controlled adult she was? This muddle would be sorted out, but for now there was little to do but invite him in. A shiver of alarm ran through her. Calm down, she told herself. Nothing is going to happen. Unable to meet his gaze, she turned back to fumble with the key, her fingers trembling as she tried to insert it in the lock.

Nic collected his helmet and bag before following as Hannah stalked briskly inside the impressive, stone-built house, tension and distress evident in her bearing. Whatever was wrong? OK, there had been an amusing mistake over his gender, but so what? Given the dire need she claimed the practice was in, what difference did it make if he was male or female? He did not understand, but clearly it mattered to his new employer. Frost by name, frosty by nature? That was his first impression on meeting her. But her emails had been warm, open…when she had thought he was a woman. Frowning, he wondered why Kirsty had kept the information to herself.

He watched as Hannah left her medical bag on a chair in the wide, slate-floored hallway and tossed her protective jacket on top. It was a beautiful house from the little he had seen, but it felt…what? Lonely, empty? A bit like Hannah, he decided, noting the way she held herself, remote and guarded. She gestured him to follow her to the kitchen and, as she set about thoroughly washing her hands and gathering things to make coffee, he stood back and observed her.

Dr Hannah Frost was younger than he had expected, around his own age, he estimated, and she was a very attractive woman in an understated way. Three or four inches shorter than himself, she moved with supple grace, and even in her coveralls he could tell her body was pleasingly curvy. A riot of long, chestnut tresses were barely restrained and tendrils had escaped a loose plait to frame an interesting and intelligent face. Her skin was creamy smooth, free of make-up, and an intriguing line of pale freckles trailed across her cheekbones and over the bridge of her nose.

It was her eyes, however, that had arrested his attention from the first. An unusual, intense green, they had a smattering of golden flecks that sparkled with her mood. And they spoke volumes, reflecting every passing emotion. In the space of their brief acquaintance she had been worried, annoyed, confused, shocked and, unless he was very much mistaken, frightened. It was the latter that troubled him the most.

At the moment she also looked dishevelled and he judged from her rumpled outfit and smudges of dirt that she had been out on a difficult call. 'Bad night?'

'You could say that.' Her tone brisk and to the point, she filled him in on the car accident she had attended. 'Whether the young man will pull through remains to be seen.'

'Let us hope so. You must be tired.'

She shrugged, keeping her gaze averted. 'I'm certainly grubby. I must go and change. Please, help yourself to coffee when it's ready and something to eat.'

Nic watched her leave the room, her back ramrod straight. He didn't understand her at all. Friendly in her emails, obviously in need of help in the practice, but now he had arrived she appeared cold and unwelcoming. Something didn't fit. A frown of consideration on his face, he examined the contents of the fridge and set about preparing breakfast.

When she returned to the kitchen half an hour later, he was unsurprised by her altered appearance. Clearly she had needed fortifying. The hair was tamed and scraped back in a severe knot. It was a shame. He had looked forward to seeing it in all its glory. Disturbed at the sudden tightening in his gut, he ruthlessly banished wayward and unwanted thoughts, the stab of desire he had not felt for two long years since… Again, he tamped down painful, dangerous thoughts and continued his assessment.

Hannah obviously thought this image made her more unapproachable while in reality it highlighted the perfection of her bone structure and the beauty of her face, the small, straight nose, the curve of pleasingly full lips, the classic jaw line. She was dressed in a smart but demure navy trouser suit, one which was well cut but neutralised her shape. He had the feeling it was a costume, her work persona, something she wore for protection, to maintain a front.

'Sit.' He smiled. 'You are hungry, no?'

It looked as if she wanted to say something, to argue, but he turned away to dish up the food, and after a moment he heard a chair scrape on the slate floor as she sat at the table. Her wary green gaze skittered from his as he crossed the room and set a plate of bacon, scrambled eggs and grilled tomatoes in front of her.

'You did this?'

Her surprise amused him. 'I am quite domesticated.' He smiled, pouring two mugs of coffee. 'Milk and sugar?'

'Just milk. Thank you.' He watched a frown crease the smoothness of her brow when she realised there was only one plate. 'Aren't you eating?'

'I had breakfast on the way.'

When she began her meal, Nic drew out a chair across from her, sensing she would be more comfortable if he did not sit too close.

'I had expected you to let us know your travel plans.'

The cool, accusing tone was back in her voice. 'I came straight from France. It seemed easier than going back to Italy and starting again. I made better time than I anticipated.'

'And your things?'

'I've organised for them to be sent on. My medical kit and essentials always travel with me. Including my papers,' he added, pushing them across the table for her to examine and confirm his identity.

He leaned back in the chair, his cup of coffee

cradled in his hands as he watched her sift through the documents, smiling when, with a small sigh, clearly unable to find anything wrong, she pushed them back to him. 'Thanks.'

'So how long have you been managing alone here?'

'Nearly three weeks.'

'It's a lot to take on for one person,' he allowed, noting the dark circles under her eyes. 'You are exhausted, no?'

She glanced towards him warily, failing to meet his gaze. 'I was more worried for my staff and patients, but it has been a difficult few weeks. It's not always like this. We were badly let down by someone, hence the urgent search for a new locum.'

'Not easy to find.'

'Indeed.'

'Then it is silly to worry whether I am male or female, no? You need help. I am here to do a job.'

'But—'

'You have a queue of other people waiting to fill the position?'

'No. No, I don't.'

Nic watched as she briefly closed her eyes. When she opened them again he caught her gaze and held it, seeing resignation and annoyance in those expressive green eyes, but a latent fear still lurked within their depths, puzzling him anew. Something was wrong. He didn't know what…not yet. But before his time here was over, he intended to find out what demons haunted this woman and what lay beneath her frosty exterior.

Hannah finished her food in silence, unwilling to admit she had been touched by his thoughtfulness preparing her a meal. She felt worn out—physically exhausted from working such long hours and mentally worn down by Nic's arguments. The hell of it was, he was right. He would have to stay. But the thought of sharing her house with him brought an ache of doubt and alarm to her stomach.

There was no way out. She could hardly ask him to make other living arrangements. Accommodation in the main house was part of the deal. Everyone knew it was how things had always been done, ever since her father's day, and both the staff and the community would find her overreaction to Nic's identity inexplicable. Given she had no intention of explaining to anyone, she would have to cope with the situation. Somehow. Either that or draw unwelcome attention to her own anxiety. And that was out of the question.

It had never been a problem before. In fact, she

had enjoyed the extra company, but most of the visiting locums had been female, or married with spouses. It was true there had been a couple of single men early on, but they had not been attracted to her, or she to them, and she had seen little of them.

She reined her thoughts in with a jerk. Where had that come from? What had attraction to do with anything? Of course she wasn't attracted to Nic. She had no intention of being attracted to anyone. Not now, not ever. And why would he be attracted to her? He barely knew her and probably had a string of girlfriends at home or left behind at his various ports of call over the last couple of years. She had been anything but welcoming and friendly so far, so all she had to do was maintain a distance, keep up her guard, and she could see this through.

'Thank you for breakfast,' she said with cool politeness. 'Perhaps I should show you to your room—if you plan to stay.'

'Oh, I'm definitely staying, *cara*.'

Hannah tried to ignore the shiver that ran through her at the knowing amusement in his reply. Conscious of him following as she led the way up the wide, curving staircase, she was glad the guest rooms were at the other end of the house to her own, and that she had thought to prepare everything in advance.

'You'll be in here,' she informed briskly, nodding across the room. 'There's an *en suite* bathroom through that door. I'll give you a set of keys for the house and surgery. And there's a file of useful local information on the dressing-table about shops, services, local attractions, that kind of thing. And maps.'

'Thank you, Hannah, I'm sure I shall be very comfortable.'

She saw his gaze take in every detail of the room. 'Good. Let me know if there is anything you need.'

'I will, believe me.'

His throaty promise, accompanied by the glint of laughter in those dark, watchful eyes had her backing towards the door. 'I'll leave you to settle in.'

'Are you on call today?' he queried, detaining her.

'No, why?'

He dropped his bag on the bed and turned to face her. 'I need a shower and a change of clothes but I thought it might be a good day for you to show me round the surgery. It will be quiet, yes?'

'Yes.' The rest of the day stretched ahead in terrifying fashion. What on earth was she going to do about him? A visit to the surgery would certainly fill in some of the time with official activities. 'A good idea.'

'Then shall I meet you downstairs in an hour or so?'

'Fine.'

Hannah felt anything but fine as, having spent an hour in the sanctuary of her room, fretting over the turn of events, she now found herself walking briskly down the road with Nic towards the surgery a mile from the house. Set in a gentle valley and surrounded by wooded hills, Lochanrig was an attractive and well-equipped village. The main street curved gently and buildings lined both sides— houses, shops, the pub, chemist, post office, Allan Pollock's garage, and at the far end from the surgery was the village school. Sheltered by the hills, it was an idyllic setting with its loch, rolling farmland, woods and the small river that flowed south, down from the hills.

'This is a very beautiful area.'

She glanced at Nic and saw he was looking around with interest. 'Yes, we are very lucky. The community might be quite scattered, but it is very friendly and close-knit.'

'I shall look forward to meeting everyone.' His dark gaze turned to her and he smiled. 'So, tell me more about how you came to be here in Lochanrig.'

'It's very much a family concern,' she explained, grateful to have something neutral to discuss. 'The practice was started by my grandfather nearly seventy years ago. My father was born here and he became a doctor, working with my grandfather and then taking over the practice. My mother was a practice nurse and worked with my father for many years. I was born here, too. The new purpose-built surgery was built ten years ago and provides a good range of facilities. After I finished my training, and with the retirement of my father's partner in the practice, I came home to take my place here.'

'You must have enjoyed working together.'

Hannah looked steadfastly ahead. 'We did. Unfortunately it was not to be for very long.'

'What happened, Hannah?' he queried after a few moments of silence, his voice soft with concern, something about the way he pronounced her name sending a disturbing shiver along her spine.

'My mother was killed in a hit-and-run accident four years ago and, sadly, my father suffered a fatal heart attack in his car a year later,' she informed him, giving the bare details but divulging nothing of the horror of events.

'I am so sorry.'

'Thank you.'

His sympathy sounded genuine, but his accompanying gesture, placing a consoling hand on her back, had her mental alarm bells clanging. Her defence mechanism springing unconsciously into action, she stepped hastily away from his touch.

She sensed his hesitation, knew he was aware of her rejection. 'And you've been running things since then?' he finally asked.

'Yes. With locum cover. And an excellent staff.'

'Do—?'

'This is the surgery,' she interrupted, thankful for an excuse to forestall further conversation. 'I'll show you the alarm system. It's key-operated but we have a code number which we change regularly.'

'You keep medications on site?'

'The usual. Patient prescriptions are obtained from the local pharmacy.'

Once inside, Nic stopped to inspect the board in the spacious reception area that displayed photos of the team of staff. 'This will help me until I remember who everyone is.'

Hannah waited while he examined the pictures, realising that the photograph of her looked severe and she was the only person not smiling. The annoying grin on his face as he turned to her raised her irritation and made her wonder if he had noticed, too.

'As you can see, we have two receptionists, including Kirsty who doubles as my practice manager. There are two district nurses, a practice nurse and a midwife.'

Nic nodded, looking back at the photographs. 'You also have support staff?'

'Yes, we can outsource anything that is needed. The physiotherapist runs a clinic here once a week and we have a counsellor who comes in two days a month,' Hannah confirmed, before moving on.

Nic's examination of the surgery was equally thorough. Appointment system, patients' records, staffroom, small kitchen, nurses' and visiting practitioner rooms, a quiet room sometimes needed for troubled patients, small play area for children, treatment room and, finally, the consulting rooms.

'You'll be in here,' Hannah said, opening the door to what had once been her father's domain. She hadn't been able to move in herself, but it no longer troubled her to have others use it.

'You have excellent facilities here,' Nic praised, walking across the room and widening the slats of the blind at the window with the fingers of one hand. 'Great views also!'

'I doubt you'll get much time to appreciate that with the patient workload we have at the moment.'

Hannah regretted her asperity when she saw one eyebrow rise and his lips quirk in a smile. 'I won't shirk my duties, I promise you.'

'Fine.' Feeling foolish, she watched as he sat at the

desk, already looking as if he belonged there, damn him! 'There will be some night and weekend calls on a rota basis, otherwise it is customary general practice work—daily surgeries, clinics and home visits. I'm arranging a car for you.'

'Thank you, Hannah.'

Ignoring the disturbing smile, she concentrated on matters at hand. 'Perhaps I should show you the computer system.'

'OK.'

Was he always so good-natured and equable? she wondered sourly, realising this had not been her best idea as she had to stand far too close to him while she ran through the standard practice procedures for recording patient details, follow-ups, requesting tests and consultations with hospitals or specialists, writing prescriptions and so on. Surely it was imagination that she could feel his body heat across the distance that separated them? She could certainly detect the sensual and disturbing aroma of his after-shave. Sandalwood, she thought. Not that she was a connoisseur of men's fragrances. This was ridiculous, she had to be losing her mind. He leaned forward, brushing against her as he experimented with some of her directions. Uncomfortable, she drew back, alarmed at how breathless she suddenly felt.

'That all seems fine,' Nic confirmed, and if he had noticed her reaction he thankfully chose to make no comment. 'I can always shout, if I get stuck.'

'Of course.'

He swivelled round in the chair, watching her. 'So, did you always want to be a GP?'

Hannah shrugged. 'I toyed with the idea of trauma once but...'

'What happened?'

'How do you mean?'

She saw Nic frown and told herself not to be so jumpy, or to imagine ulterior motives where none existed.

'I just wondered why you had come back here to be a GP.'

'Mum and Dad needed me. The practice needed me.'

'And what did you need?'

To be safe, she admitted to herself, but no way was she telling him that. 'I just need to do my job.'

'You are not what I expected.'

'Excuse me?' Hannah bristled.

'I imagined someone in sole charge of running a practice like this would be older.'

'I'm a good doctor.'

'I don't doubt your abilities, Hannah,' he replied,

a thread of chastisement in his voice. 'I meant simply that the responsibility must have been hard for you, especially in the circumstances, when your loss was so raw.'

Hannah swallowed down a prickle of emotion at his sympathetic understanding. 'I just did what was necessary in order to carry on. That's all any of us can do, isn't it?'

'Yes. It is.'

His words were soft, laced with unexpected emotion. Hannah's gaze met his and she nearly gasped at the anguish that bruised his dark eyes before he blinked and looked away from her. What had happened in his own life to cause him such pain? Questions hovered but remained unasked. Aside from the fact that she hated people questioning her about her personal life, she had no wish to come to know Nic more closely, or to find more common ground with him than their shared profession.

'Is there anything else you wish to see here?' she asked instead, determined to draw things back to a more comfortable level.

'No.' He rose to his feet with the sinuous grace of a jungle cat. 'Let's go.'

'What made you interested in spending time in a

small rural practice in Scotland?' Hannah queried as they walked back to the house.

'My mama's father was a Scot and I have always wanted to spend some time in his country. The remoteness does not concern me,' he reassured her with a smile, looking towards the hills with an expression of contentment on his face. 'I feel sure my stay in Lochanrig will provide me with all the challenges I need, both in my working life and whatever leisure time is available to me. I love to walk, cycle, climb…' His dark gaze met hers. 'There will be plenty here to hold my attention.'

Hannah hoped he didn't for a moment imagine turning any of his attention onto her. She mulled over his words with a frown, thankful that she saw little of Nic for the rest of the afternoon. He went for a walk, familiarising himself with the village, and then spent time in his room, apparently looking at the local maps and other information she had left for him. It was only when he came downstairs and joined her in the kitchen that she realised with alarm that the whole evening still stretched ahead of them.

'If you have plans to go out, don't let me being here stop you,' he remarked, as if reading her mind.

'Pardon?'

'A date or anything.'

'No, no, I—'

She snapped off her words. There was no way she was going to tell him that she didn't do dates, that she had no real social life to speak of. But now she was stuck here. Why on earth hadn't she just agreed and used the excuse to escape for a while? And go where, to do what? she taunted herself. Sit in the car in the dark?

Instead, she found herself preparing bowls of home-made soup, which they ate at the kitchen table with fresh, chunky bread and then fresh fruit to follow. Several times she was aware of him watching her and felt her tension and awareness increase. Unable to prevent it, her gaze strayed to him. He sat with his head resting on one hand, his fingers sunk in the thickness of his hair. For a crazy moment she had the compelling urge to run her own fingers through it. What would it feel like against her skin? She looked away hastily, getting herself under control. What on earth was the matter with her? And why did he keep looking at her like that? The rest of the evening was going to be torture at this rate.

Uncomfortable, Hannah cleared her throat. 'How come you speak English so fluently?' she asked, searching for some safe subject to break the diffi-cult silence.

'My grandpapa encouraged my mama to speak English from childhood and she did the same for me.'

They chatted for a while about the village and Hannah filled him in on the staff and information on some of their regular patients and more tricky cases. But all the while she felt on edge, unsettled, far too aware of her unwelcome new house guest and colleague. She was relieved when the telephone rang and she rose to her feet.

'Excuse me.'

His meal finished, Nic watched as Hannah moved to the phone in the hall. What flustered her so much? She had been on edge all day, had never relaxed or lost that flicker of fear that shadowed her eyes.

'Anything wrong?' he asked when she returned to the kitchen, a frown on her face.

'I have to go out after all.'

'I thought you weren't on call.'

'I'm not, officially, but that was Dr Robert MacKenzie, who is cover for tonight. He's stuck with a difficult birth about fifteen miles away and now there's an urgent call to a sick child just down the road,' she explained, pulling on her coat. 'It's easier if I go.'

Nic rose to his feet. 'I'll come with you.'

'But—'

'I have to start work some time.'

He could see she wasn't pleased but she wasted no more time arguing. Grabbing his bag and his jacket, he joined her at the car.

'These are patients of yours?' he questioned once they were on their way.

'Yes. Claire Carlyle is a single mum in her early twenties. She doesn't call us out for nothing. She has two children, Tom, who is six, and Faye, who is two. It's the little girl we're going to see.'

'And Claire, has she anyone to help?'

'No. Her parents threw her out when she was expecting Tom.'

Nic heard the frustration and disapproval in her voice. 'And the boyfriend?'

'Took off with someone else about six months ago.'

'Charming.' Nic scowled, sharing the anger and sympathy Hannah betrayed. 'It sounds as if she's had a hard time.'

'Indeed. We're here.'

Nic followed as Hannah led the way up a grubby flight of stairs in a grey, bleak building to a flat on the second floor. The door stood ajar and she pushed it open and went in, calling Claire's name. A harassed, anxious-looking girl greeted them. She looked anaemic and in need of a good meal, Nic assessed, concerned at her thinness and her pallor.

'Oh, Dr Frost, I'm so sorry to trouble you,' the girl cried, wringing her hands in agitation. 'Faye's been poorly all afternoon and I just got scared.'

'It's all right, Claire, you did the right thing,' Hannah soothed, surprising Nic with her complete change in manner.

'She's through here. I didn't know what to do. A neighbour has had Tom in to play with her kids.'

They followed the worried mother through the untidy flat to a tiny back bedroom where the young child grizzled in a cot. Hannah set down her bag and took off her coat, glancing towards him.

'Claire, this is Dr di Angelis, he's going to be working with the practice for a while.'

Frightened blue eyes met his. 'Oh, OK.'

'Hello, Claire.' He smiled, stepping forward. 'I know you must be scared but we'll do our best to help your little one. May I take a look at her?'

He sensed Hannah's surprise, but his focus was on the young mother. When she nodded, he smiled again and, opening his bag, took out his stethoscope and digital thermometer, asking a few questions as he readied himself.

'Faye has had a fever?'

'Yes,' Claire confirmed. 'And she's been crying and crying.'

'Has she vomited at all? Got a rash?'

Claire nodded. 'She's been sick a couple of times. But she hasn't got an actual rash. I just didn't know what to do.'

'You were right to call us,' Hannah reassured again.

'Poor *bambina*.' Nic soothed the fractious child, frowning as he made a thorough assessment. The skin was blotchy, although there was no sign of the purpura rash often associated with meningitis. The child's breathing was rapid, though, and she exhibited some joint stiffness, along with photophobia, resistance to light. Concerned, he looked up and met Hannah's gaze, his voice soft. 'Call an ambulance, please.'

'Do you think it is meningitis?' Claire fretted as Hannah took out her mobile phone and made the call without question.

'It is better to be safe than sorry.' Nic spoke softly, trying not to alarm the young woman unduly. 'The signs are worrying and I would feel happier if Faye is properly checked out. OK? Is your daughter allergic to penicillin?'

Claire shook her head, seeming uncertain. 'I don't think so. No.'

'Good. We will give her an injection now and then she will be transferred to hospital.'

'Can I go with her?'

'Yes, of course.'

'The ambulance is on its way,' Hannah announced, turning to Claire with a smile. 'Would you like me to help you pack a few things you might need to take with you? Dr di Angelis will look after Faye.'

Tears escaping down her pale cheeks, Claire nodded. As Hannah ushered her out, Nic returned his attention to the sick child, administering the injection of penicillin, hoping they had caught things in time.

Twenty minutes later they returned home, Faye safely on her way to hospital, a frightened Claire accompanying her in the ambulance, and the neighbour promising to care for Tom.

'Poor girl,' Nic sighed as he followed Hannah indoors.

'You were very good with her.'

Nic smiled at Hannah's unexpected praise, even if it had been delivered in those cool, controlled tones. 'Thank you.'

'Coffee?'

'Please. Shall I make it?' he volunteered, moving towards her.

'It's OK.'

She stepped quickly away from him and busied herself with the task, keeping her back to him. He had learned something this evening, Nic reflected, a frown of consideration on his face as he leant against the counter and watched her. Doctor Hannah and private Hannah appeared to be two very different personalities. She had been softer, warmer with her patients. And it was the first time he had seen her smile. It had been as if someone had switched a light on inside her, transforming her whole face, and it had brought a flicker of awareness inside him. As soon as the ambulance had left, though, she had gone back to her serious, prickly self. Now she seemed paralysed by discomfort. Was it just him, or was she like this with other people? Intrigued, he vowed to unravel the mysteries of this woman in the days and weeks ahead.

He accepted the coffee she handed him and smiled as he gently chinked their mugs together. 'Here's to our new partnership.'

Varied emotions chased each other across those expressive eyes. Doubt, annoyance, resignation… but always that underlying shadow of fear that troubled him.

'Drink up,' he instructed, keeping his tone light and teasing. 'It looks as if you are stuck with me, Hannah!'

'So it would seem—for now,' she allowed, her voice cool, her reluctance and disapproval evident. 'Welcome to Lochanrig, Dr di Angelis.'

A slow smile curved his mouth. 'Thank you, Dr Frost. I'm sure my stay here with you is going to be a very interesting one indeed. For both of us.'

CHAPTER THREE

'KIRSTY, this is our new doctor, Nic di Angelis,' Hannah announced brusquely as she walked towards the reception desk at the surgery on Monday morning, Nic close behind her.

She had the satisfaction of seeing the surprise and chagrin on her practice manager's face as Kirsty's gaze slid guiltily from hers and towards Nic. Clearing her throat, the older woman smiled.

'Hello, Nic, nice to have you join us.' Kirsty's welcome was accompanied by a rare broad smile. 'We didn't expect you so soon.'

'So I have discovered.' Hannah bristled as Nic flicked her a grin before returning his attention to Kirsty and shaking hands. 'It is a pleasure to meet you, also.'

Hannah looked on with a scowl as her usually straight-talking manager, wary of new people, simpered over their new doctor. 'Kirsty, I'm sure Nic doesn't need babysitting, so I suggest we divide up the morning surgery and you pass some consultations over to him. Is that all right with you, Nic?' she added as politely as she could.

'Fine, *cara*,' he replied, amusement glittering in his eyes. 'It is nice to know you have confidence in my skills.'

'I don't think your competence as a doctor has ever been in doubt.'

Looking from one to the other, clearly aware of the tension, Kirsty's eyebrows rose. 'Is everything all right?'

'Fine,' Hannah stated before Nic could speak, planning to take her manager to task in private. 'It will be a week or two before we have a car for you, so I suggest you accompany me on some house calls to learn the lie of the land.'

'I shall be delighted, Hannah,' Nic agreed with a mock-solicitousness that set her teeth on edge.

'It would also be a good idea if you went out with the district nurses sometimes.' The more often the better, she added silently, welcoming the prospect of getting rid of him. 'Kirsty, perhaps you could arrange that? And assisting with some of the clinics?'

'Of course. What about a staff meeting?'

Hannah frowned. 'A staff meeting?'

'To introduce Nic to everyone,' Kirsty tutted.

'I see. Well…' Hannah floundered, uncomfortably aware of Nic's amused gaze on her and of her own desperate need to put some distance between them. 'Yes, I suppose that would be a good idea,' she allowed grudgingly. 'Perhaps you could see to it?'

'My pleasure.' Kirsty grinned.

Hannah was relieved to have matters settled. 'Fine. Now, can we check the patient list and see who can go where?'

With Nic standing far too close, Hannah inched away and tried to concentrate on the task at hand, dividing up the morning appointments. She glanced at his profile while he was occupied talking with Kirsty. He had the kind of eyelashes many women paid good money to fake. They were long and lustrous, fringing eyes the colour of rich, melted chocolate, warm and tempting… Dear God! Whatever had come over her?

'Hannah?'

She blinked and realised both Kirsty and Nic were staring at her. 'I'm sorry, I was thinking about something,' she excused herself, warmth washing her face as she avoided Nic's gaze.

'I asked if you were happy with the assignment of the morning list,' Kirsty repeated, a quizzical expression on her face.

'Yes, of course,' Hannah said. She hadn't been following the discussion at all. What had happened to her in the last twenty-four hours? Why had Nic's arrival addled her brain? Pulling herself together, she picked up her box of notes and stepped back. 'Shall we get on, then?'

Smiling at Kirsty, Nic collected his own pile of notes and turned to follow her. 'We set to work, Hannah.'

'Let me know if you have any problems.'

'Don't worry,' he chided softly as they paused outside the door of her consulting room. Holding her gaze for a long moment, his own expression intense, he touched one finger to the tip of her nose before walking on towards his own door. 'Everything will be fine.'

Escaping to the privacy of her room, she closed the door and leant back against it for a moment, wondering what Nic had meant. She sensed there was much more behind his words than the success of morning surgery. Her legs unusually shaky, Hannah crossed to her desk and sat down. Disturbed at the way her skin still tingled, she rubbed her hand over her nose, wanting to erase the unexpected and unwanted feel of his touch. Why had he done that? Why did he appear so in control while her whole world had suddenly spun horribly out of kilter?

Picking up the telephone, she called through to Reception. 'Kirsty, I'd like a word in my room, please.'

A rap on the door announced Kirsty's arrival a few moments later. Hannah glanced up and beckoned her in.

'I've introduced Nic to Morag,' Kirsty informed her before Hannah could begin her inquisition. 'As practice nurse, she's going to be available should he need a chaperone for any consultations.'

Hannah frowned, knowing she should have thought of that herself. 'Thank you, Kirsty. Sit down, please,' she invited, tension roiling within her.

'Hannah—'

Unprepared to be mollified before she had even had her say, Hannah held up her hand. 'Why did you continue to allow me to believe our new locum was female even after you had spoken to Nic on the telephone? When exactly did you plan to tell me? It was very embarrassing, being confronted on my own doorstep and having no idea who he was.'

'I planned to tell you before he arrived. I wasn't expecting him to be here until today or tomorrow. I'm sorry if that caused you any difficulties—that wasn't my intention,' Kirsty said, not looking as contrite as Hannah would have wished.

'So what was your intention?'

'To obtain an excellent locum doctor for the practice.'

Hannah's eyebrows rose. 'And you think I don't want the same thing?' she challenged, her annoyance growing.

'Listen, Hannah. We were in a desperate situation and having you working beyond endurance alone was impacting not only on your own health but also on your patients and all the rest of the staff,' Kirsty explained, not mincing her words. 'You have to admit that you find all manner of excuses to avoid employing men, and if I had told you last week that Nicola di Angelis was a man, you would have done the same thing, holding out who knows how long in the hope of finding another woman locum. Well, I'm sorry, but we didn't have the luxury of going through all that,' she continued mercilessly. 'Locums are hard to find, good ones are like gold dust. I don't know what the issue is, it isn't my business unless it affects work, but my duty is to the well-being of the whole practice, has been so for the twenty years I worked for your parents and now for you. I did what I thought was right for everyone, for the sake of the patients and the rest of us, and I suggest that whatever your problem is, you put it aside once and for all and appreciate what an excellent doctor we have for the next six months.'

Shocked, Hannah closed her eyes, feeling both furious and chastened, unable to deal with the underlying issues to which Kirsty referred, scared her practice manager had struck too close to the bone, that she had allowed her own personal prejudices to adversely affect her professional judgement.

'Hannah?' Kirsty sounded concerned, her voice softer. 'I'm sorry.'

'I appreciate you were acting out of concern for the practice but I would be grateful if you would not keep things from me in future,' she managed, stiff with tension, unable to meet her manager's all-seeing gaze.

'Of course.'

Clasping her hands together on her lap, Hannah took a deep breath. 'That will be all. Please, send the first patient in when you are ready.'

'Sure,' Kirsty agreed, but it was clear from her tone her feathers had been ruffled by the terse dismissal.

'If you get a minute, could you phone the hospital and see if there is any news on little Faye Carlyle? She was admitted last night with suspected meningitis.'

'Oh, no, poor Claire,' Kirsty sympathised with concern, her strop forgotten. 'She's had a lot to deal with, that girl. I'll let you know if there's any news.'

'Thanks.'

Trying to set her confrontation with Kirsty and her jumbled thoughts about Nic aside, Hannah switched on her computer, straightened her desk and prepared for her first patient.

Morning surgery was finished in half the usual time and, as far as Hannah knew, Nic had not experienced any problems. Relieved, she lingered in her consulting room far longer than was necessary, unaccountably nervous about joining the others. Eventually, unable to delay any longer, she slipped into the staffroom as surreptitiously as possible, but as she poured herself a cup of coffee, the hairs on the back of her neck prickled and she knew Nic was looking at her.

'What part of Italy are you from, Nic?' Shona Brown, one of the district nurses, asked him.

'The region of Umbria. A small village between Assisi and the Le Marche border,' he informed.

'But you've been working in various places, haven't you?' Kirsty questioned. 'You were in Canada, as well as the UK?'

'Yes, I have enjoyed my travels and new experiences.'

His response was friendly, but Hannah sensed his discomfort answering questions about himself. Maybe she recognised it because she shared it? Either way, she found herself stepping in, assuring herself it was because she was impatient to return to work.

'Are you ready for house calls, Nic?'

'I need just a moment to collect my things,' he replied, rising to his feet and washing his mug at the sink. 'I'll meet you outside.'

'Fine.'

As he left the room, Hannah finished her coffee and washed her own mug, uncomfortable at the excited chat around her.

'Wow! He's amazing,' Debbie enthused.

'And very good with the patients,' Morag said approvingly. 'I went in to help on a couple of occasions and was very impressed.'

'We've certainly hit the jackpot this time,' Kirsty declared with satisfaction, her tone raising Hannah's hackles again, but everyone else chorused their agreement on Nic's virtues.

Irritated, Hannah tossed down the teatowel she had used to dry her mug and turned to leave. She certainly didn't want to keep hearing how wonderful Nic was, or join some unofficial fan club for the man!

'Don't you like him, Hannah?' Jane asked. 'He seems so lovely.'

The young receptionist's soft enquiry startled her. She hadn't realised her antipathy was so apparent.

Aware they were all waiting for her answer, Hannah shrugged. 'I've not really thought about it,' she fibbed. 'As long as he's a good doctor, that's all that matters.'

Disgruntled, she left the room to collect her coat, bag and the notes she needed for the home visits. It seemed Nic had charmed everyone in the short time he had been there. And it was genuine, not just an act. He was simply a nice man. Which made it even more important for her to keep up her guard, she decided, afraid that she could be in danger of liking him far too much.

Nic leant against the car, waiting for Hannah to join him. He suspected she had understood his discomfort with talking about himself back there. But he sensed they were two of a kind, not that she would ever admit that, he knew. He had no idea why she had buried herself in her work, what she was hiding from, but he recognised it because he had done the same these past two years.

He straightened as Hannah left the surgery and walked briskly towards him, dressed in a sober dark grey trouser suit, her hair restrained as usual in a tight plait. There was a grim expression on her face that didn't bode well for an easing of the atmosphere between them. He wondered if she had any idea how expressive those amazing eyes were. It was doubtful.

She would hate to know he could tell pretty much everything she was thinking. He chuckled.

'Is something funny?'

Realising his chuckle must have been audible, he glanced at her and saw her fiery expression. 'No, Hannah, I was just thinking of something.'

She looked at him suspiciously for a moment. 'I thought you would like to know that Kirsty has been in touch with the hospital and Faye Carlyle does have meningitis but is responding to treatment.'

'That's great.' Nic smiled with relief. 'I hope she comes through without any lasting problems.'

'Indeed.'

As Hannah drove out of the car park and headed away from the village, Nic tried to stop thinking about her and turn his attention to the work ahead. 'Where are we going?'

'To see Joanne McStay and her mother,' Hannah informed him. 'Mrs McStay has been poorly for a long time with Alzheimer's disease. She's quite frail now and difficult at times. Joanne gave up an option to go to university to get a job and stay at home to care for her mother. This last year she's had to give up the job as well.'

'And there's no other family to help?'

'No.'

Nic thought quietly for a moment. 'So are we going to see Joanne, Mrs McStay or both?'

'Both,' she agreed, and he noticed her flicker of surprise. 'Why?'

'You seem rightly as concerned for Joanne as for her mama. It must be very hard for her.'

'It is. She's very isolated and I don't have as much time to give her as I would like.'

'Why don't you let me have a chat with Joanne while you see her mama?'

He saw her frown as she considered his suggestion. 'What do you have in mind?'

'I'll talk to her about things we can do to help. What options are available here? Is there help at home? How about respite care?'

'Believe me, I've tried,' Hannah assured him, frustration in her voice as she explained what was available locally and the choices she had already discussed. 'Joanne won't hear of it.'

Nic said no more as they arrived at the small cottage on the outskirts of a nearby village. As they waited at the front door, he heard bolts being undone before it was finally opened and they were being shown inside by a tall, thin girl who looked on the point of exhaustion.

'Joanne, this is Dr di Angelis.' Hannah introduced

them with a smile for the girl. 'He's just joined the practice for a short while.'

'Hello.'

Joanne's voice was listless but Nic smiled and shook her hand, finding her skin cool and dry to the touch. 'Nice to meet you, Joanne.'

'How have things been?' Hannah asked, taking off her coat and draping it over a chair.

'A bit grim,' the girl allowed, her voice flat. 'We had a bad night. Mum was up a lot, trying to get out, and she wouldn't settle. She's been asleep this morning, though.'

'You look as if you could do with a good sleep yourself, Joanne.' Hannah smiled sympathetically.

The girl gave a mirthless laugh. 'Not much chance of that, Doctor.'

Nic met Hannah's concerned gaze. 'Joanne, Dr Frost is going to see your mama, and we'll sit here and have a chat about things—is that all right?'

Joanne looked puzzled and awkward as she gazed from one to the other. 'Well, I suppose so...'

'I won't be long. I know the way.' Hannah smiled, picked up her bag and left the room.

Encouraging the girl to sit down, Nic took a place on the shabby sofa next to her. 'Things must be very hard for you. It's not easy, is it, caring for someone?'

'No.' Joanne's chin wobbled. 'But she's my mum. I can't just leave her.'

'I understand and I think you are doing a great job, but there are things we can do to help make it easier for you.'

'She doesn't want strangers coming in to her. I ought to be able to manage,' she cried, tears slipping between her lashes.

Nic handed her a tissue. 'It's not wrong to need help, Joanne. Neither is it wrong to feel resentful or angry at your mama and the situation you are in. It all seems very unfair sometimes, no?'

'I feel so selfish and guilty,' she admitted, crying openly now.

'That is normal,' Nic soothed, holding her hand. 'It is a very difficult thing you are doing and it doesn't mean you care less.' He looked up as Hannah came quietly back into the room and sat down, a look of amazement on her face. 'Dr Frost has told me you've been coping so well in desperately difficult circumstances.'

'I just don't know what to do. Sometimes I don't think I can cope any more,' the girl sobbed, accepting a fresh tissue.

'You don't have to cope on your own. But if you don't take care of yourself, of your own health, you are not going to be able to help either your mama or yourself, no?'

'I suppose not.' She looked up at them. 'Sometimes I think it would be better if Mum went into care, but I promised her I wouldn't let that happen.'

'We don't have to do that, Joanne, not for a while anyway, but the choices are getting fewer, you know that,' Hannah told her softly.

Joanne nodded, her hazel eyes sad. 'What can I do, then?'

'You need to think about yourself, for a little while at least,' Nic advised. 'If you allowed us to arrange some respite care, just for a week or two, your mama would be well cared for and you could have a break, even go away for a holiday. You would feel so much better and more able to cope when you came back.'

'Do you think so?' Joanne asked, a flicker of hope on her face.

Hannah smiled at her. 'I'm sure of it. And when you come back we can make sure you have some daily help and more regular breaks. How does that sound?'

'Amazing!' she admitted, laughing and sniffing at the same time.

'And you don't have to be alone,' Nic advised, glancing at Hannah for confirmation. 'There is a support group where you can be in touch with other carers coping with Alzheimer's, who will understand what you are going through, is that not right, Dr Frost?'

'It is. A local group would help, Joanne, and there are national ones, too.'

'Thanks.' Joanne wiped her eyes and gave a watery smile. 'OK. Will you see what's available? I thought I could cope, but it is getting so much harder.'

'We'll do all we can to help you, Joanne,' Hannah promised.

Nic rose to his feet, assisting Hannah with her coat, noting how swiftly she moved away from him. Filing the moment away for another time, he turned to smile again at Joanne. 'You can always ring the surgery if you need anything or you just want to talk.'

'Thank you both. I feel much better.'

Holding her bag in front of her, like a shield, Nic thought, Hannah walked towards the front door. 'Your mum's still sleeping, Joanne, so I've not disturbed her. You have a rest while you can and we'll be in touch soon with some proposals for you, and someone will pop back in a day or two to see your mum.'

Back in the car, Hannah was quiet for a while as she drove them away from the McStays' cottage. They had covered a couple of miles before she threw him a brief glance, curiosity and puzzlement in her eyes.

'I don't know what you did, but thank you for bringing Joanne round.'

'Let's hope it works for her.'

They had several other routine house calls and Nic used the time not only to begin to know more of his new patient base but also to observe Hannah at work, impressed with her professionalism, her skills as a doctor and her rapport with her patients. As they returned to the surgery in time for lunch, he wondered again at the two very different sides to her character.

'Feel free to go home and eat if you want to,' Hannah offered, turning her car into its parking place. 'The village has a good bakery or a pub if you prefer.'

He undid his seat belt and turned to look at her. 'And what do you do?'

'I usually just have a sandwich at my desk. Plenty of paperwork to do,' she added, sounding as if she was trying to be casual.

'Hannah?'

'What?'

He waited in silence until she reluctantly turned her head and met his gaze, her green eyes anxious.

'Why are you afraid?'

'I'm not,' she refuted, her eyes betraying her words. 'I don't know what you mean.'

'I think you do. I've known you a little more than twenty-four hours but I can see what a good doctor you are, that you give yourself to your patients and care deeply about people. But you don't let anyone close to you, do you? Not to the private Hannah.'

Her hands tightened on the steering-wheel, her knuckles whitening. 'I have a busy and fulfilling career, security. I don't need anything or anyone else in my life.'

'Why?'

'It's just the way I am.'

'Or the way you have become?'

He knew he had touched a raw nerve by the flash of temper that momentarily replaced the fear in her eyes. 'You are not here to psychoanalyse me, Dr di Angelis,' she snapped, gathering her things together and reaching for the doorhandle.

'I don't want to be your therapist, Hannah.'

She glanced back at him, confused, troubled. 'Then what do you want?'

'To be your friend.'

'Well, you can't.' If anything, his words served only to increase her alarm. Dragging her startled gaze from his, she flung open the door and all but scrambled out. 'Excuse me, I have work to do.'

He walked beside her towards the building, sensing her tension and discomfort. 'Of course. It's always work, isn't it? Especially when the going gets tough. But believe me, Hannah, it doesn't make things better or take the pain away.'

'Just do the job you came here for, Nic, and leave me alone.'

He watched her go, concerned at the suspicion of moisture in her eyes, the constant battle she had to keep up the coldness and the front. Her inner pain and loneliness were almost palpable to him and, whatever her protests, there was no way he was going to turn his back on that. Pain was something he was all too familiar with. He closed his eyes, fighting down his own memories, his own nightmare. The sting of pain was mellowing, he realised, but he would never forget.

Two years was a long time, and he'd moved about since then, afraid to put down roots again. He hadn't been involved with a woman in all that time, he hadn't been interested. But meeting Hannah had brought back emotions and desires he'd thought lost for ever. Now, for the first time, he was attracted to another woman. Not just attracted, he admitted with a self-mocking smile. From the moment he had first seen her, Hannah had stirred his senses and brought desire stabbing back to him.

Perhaps he had pushed too hard too soon today, but he could tell that Hannah was special, and she was hurting. Slowly but surely, he was going to use this time here to help them both to heal.

Still smarting and unsettled after her confrontation with Nic in the car on Monday, Hannah did her best to stay out of his way as much as possible, both at the surgery and at home, as the week progressed. The times he had been out to house calls with her, or when he had insisted on accompanying her on any night calls until he could do them alone, he had been polite and friendly, and there had been no more probing questions. She should have been relieved, but Nic didn't have to say anything to make her feel uncomfortable and out of sorts. He accomplished that just by existing. It was silly, but she couldn't help feeling a bit miffed at how swiftly he had fitted in, how popular he had become with both staff and patients. Kirsty, usually cautious about people until they had proved themselves, had taken to Nic from the beginning, clearly feeling justified by her own role in securing his employment.

'We've had people making appointments who've not seen a doctor for years,' she said, beaming when Hannah returned to the surgery late on Friday morning.

Hannah frowned. 'I don't understand.'

'Nic. Having a male doctor again. Some people prefer it.'

'No one said anything to me.'

'Well, they wouldn't, Hannah,' the other woman pointed out gently, making her think again of their confrontation on Monday. 'They all like and respect you so much.'

Disturbed, Hannah collected her patient notes and messages before seeking the privacy of her consulting room. Was Kirsty right? And what was it about Nic that made people trust him so rapidly, to feel they could unburden themselves? He wasn't just a pretty face, he was also an exceedingly good doctor, an asset to the practice.

She started when a tap on her door drew her from her reverie and she sat back nervously as Nic came into her room. How could she have forgotten he was already here, taking early surgery?

'Have you got a minute?' he asked, his expression thoughtful.

'I have now,' she replied briskly, trying to get her

wayward thoughts back under control, 'but I have the health board meeting this afternoon.'

'I hadn't forgotten.'

He smiled, one of those half amused, half knowing smiles that brought a knot of unfamiliar awareness to her stomach. Unbidden, her gaze lingered on his mouth. The breath locked in her throat as she helplessly studied the sensual curve of his lips. That mouth was sinful.

'What can I do for you?' she managed, her voice more fractured than usual.

'Do we have access to sex therapy?'

Momentarily startled, her mind completely on the wrong path, Hannah bristled. 'Are you trying to be funny?'

'Excuse me?' A rare flash of annoyance glinted in his eyes. 'Far from it, Hannah. I am trying my best to help a troubled patient who is waiting in my consulting room as we speak.'

She blushed, chastened and embarrassed, and turned to search for a card in her desk drawer. 'Sarah Baxter is our visiting counsellor. She'll know of a specialist and can either refer your patient on or you can discuss it with her at her clinic next week'

'Thank you.'

His tone was cool, the look her gave her so penetrating that it made her cringe. She hated it when he looked at her like that, as if he could see right inside her soul. And she feared he saw too damn much. Tense, expecting him to make some further comment, she was surprised when he took the card from her and turned away without another word, quietly closing the door behind him.

Hannah buried her head in her hands. Why did she keep doing and saying all the wrong things around him? Something about Nic made her act out of character and feel things, think things she had never wanted or expected to feel or think about. Things she had suppressed for a long, long time, ever since… No! She was *not* going there. Had she learned none of the lessons of the past? She had moved on, found her niche, made her choices. So why was her body now letting her down? Why was she starting to feel things for Nic which she knew to be a lie?

Trying to concentrate on her patients over her lunchtime surgery was difficult, but Hannah was determined not to allow Nic to invade every area of her existence. She was soon involved with a list of usual complaints from stomach upsets to skin problems, worries about a mystery lump for which she arranged an emergency referral, and then an elderly lady with a persistent leg ulcer.

She was relieved when her final consultation came to an end. 'Come and see me again next week, Moira, and we'll see how things are looking then.'

'I will, Dr Frost, and thank you.'

Hannah opened the door to show the patient out just as Nic walked by.

'Is that the new doctor?' Moira asked, after Nic had smiled at them and closed the door of his room.

'Yes, that's right.'

'Italian, I understand. I've heard he's very good. He certainly looks a picture, doesn't he?' She grinned. 'If that's what eating spaghetti and lasagne does for a man, my Ray will be having a rapid change of diet!'

Hannah forced a smile, hiding her irritation as Moira hurried back to Reception to make another appointment and no doubt have a good gossip, she thought with a grimace. What was wrong with everyone in this place? The man had been there a week and all the female population were falling over him. Feeling grumpy and unwilling to acknowledge her own confused feelings where Nic was concerned, she returned to her desk. She had time to mark up her notes and check her emails before it was time to leave for her meeting.

Opening her inbox a while later, she was surprised to find an email waiting for her from Nic. She imagined him sitting in the nearby room, writing to her, and a warm tingle ran through her. Did he know how uncomfortable she was feeling around him? Of course he did. She frowned. He seemed sensitive to everything she was thinking, and it troubled her. Anxious this was going to be about their embarrassing misunderstanding earlier, Hannah tentatively opened the message.

'Do you like pasta?'

A half-smile on her face, she emailed back. *'Yes.'*

Seconds later, a new message arrived. *'Mushrooms?'*

'Not keen. Why?'

'Wait and see!'

She was perversely disappointed there were no further messages but, pressed for time, she dealt with a couple of other emails then logged off and, after briefly stopping at Reception to leave some notes and correspondence with Jane, Hannah set off for her appointment, leaving Nic to handle the last surgery of the day.

The meeting ran on longer than expected and it was after seven when she arrived home, tired and cold. She opened the front door, hearing soft music coming from the kitchen and a delicious aroma filling the air. Frowning, she left her case on the hall chair, hung up her coat and walked to the kitchen door. Dressed in jeans and a jumper, Nic was relaxing at the table, reading a medical journal. He glanced up when she hesitated in the doorway and, closing the magazine, he smiled.

'Hi.'

'You've cooked?' Belatedly, she realised what the emails had been for.

'My speciality. Hungry?'

She was about to deny it, but her stomach betrayed her, giving an audible rumble. Embarrassed, she glanced at Nic and saw his eyes crinkle at the corners as he laughed.

'I think that was a yes,' he said, the intensity of his gaze making her feel both shy and wary.

'Have I got time to change?'

'Of course. How long?'

'Ten minutes?'

'No problem.'

As he rose effortlessly to his feet, Hannah backed out of the door and ran up the stairs. By the time she walked more slowly back down, after a hurried wash and change of clothes, Nic was dishing up the pasta. The table had been laid. He'd even found a candle and lit it, she noticed, suddenly nervous about why he had gone to so much trouble. As he turned to place a dish on the table he stopped and stared at her.

Heat washed through her under the scrutiny of his dark gaze and she shifted anxiously. 'What's wrong?' she queried uneasily.

'Nothing.' She saw him swallow before he looked away from her to set the dish down then he turned back to face her, his slow smile tightening her stomach. 'Nothing, *cara*. I wondered how many days it would be before you relaxed a bit and gave up the power suit morning, noon and night.'

Hannah glanced down in surprise, shocked to discover she had pulled on jeans and a russet-coloured fleece top without thinking, the kind of things she wore off duty when she was alone, although her hair was still held back in its braid.

'I—'

'Don't,' he interrupted. 'It suits you. Sit, yes? The food is ready.'

Uncertain, Hannah sat at the table, sipping a glass of water. She felt ridiculously panicky. What did Nic want of her? she fretted. He was an excellent doctor, seemed to be a compassionate and thoughtful man...but he was a dangerous one. She would do well to remember that and not let her guard down.

'This is delicious, thank you,' she murmured politely once Nic had sat down across from her and they had started their meal.

'My pleasure.'

Was it her imagination, or did his voice sound even more husky and intimate than usual? Studiously keeping her gaze averted, she searched for something safe to talk about, filling him in on some details from the health meeting, realising she was chattering nervously.

She took another hasty swallow of water. 'Everything OK at afternoon surgery?'

'Yes, fine. Hannah, let's not—'

'I'm sorry about this morning,' she rushed on, without thinking.

Out of the corner of her eye she saw Nic frown. 'This morning?'

'Yes, your patient. It's just we don't get much call for that sort of thing.'

'What sort of thing?'

Dear God, what had she done now? 'Um…relationship counselling. I mean…' The words trailed off when she discovered she now had Nic's full attention. Oh, damnation!

'Sex sort of things?'

'Well, yes.' Her heart started thudding uncomfortably against her ribs. Please, please, let the floor open up and swallow her. 'We've not had much demand for that sort of therapy in Lochanrig.'

'I see.'

Did he? She hoped to God he didn't. 'Well, it's just a mechanical act of procreation after all. Nothing to get so bothered about,' she dismissed, her voice heavy with cynicism. She'd never believed all that rubbish about the earth moving and stars exploding. After all, she had experienced how wrong all that nonsense was. Just lies and— Hannah suddenly realised that Nic was staring at her with a look of astonishment on his face, the fork in his hand suspended part way to his mouth. 'What's the matter?'

With careful deliberation he lowered the fork back to his plate, puffing out his cheeks as he released a long, unsteady breath. '*Madre del Dio*,' he muttered, his shocked gaze sliding away from hers.

'Nic?'

'Hannah, I—' He cleared his throat, the fingers of one hand running across his forehead as if he was trying to get his thoughts straight. '*Cara*, are you ser—?'

Whatever he had been about to say was interrupted by the telephone. Shaking his head, he seemed pleased to get away from her as he hurried from the table, and Hannah listened as he talked briefly to the caller, before coming back to the kitchen holding his medical bag.

'I have to go.'

'Do you want me to drive you?'

'No!' he refused, rather too hurriedly, she thought. 'It's a man from an outlying farm bringing someone in with a bad cut. Sounds like stitching is needed. I'm meeting them at the surgery.'

Grateful for the reprieve, she smiled. 'OK. Well, thanks for dinner. It's lovely.'

'Hannah.'

Her tentative smile faded as he walked towards her. 'What?' she murmured, wishing she didn't sound so shaky.

He stopped beside her, his dark gaze burning into hers, and she clenched her hands together in her lap to stop them trembling. 'We'll talk about this another time.'

Over her dead body, she thought, but he silenced any further words and trapped the breath inside her as he reached out and ran a finger across her cheek before turning away and leaving the house.

Hannah swallowed the uncomfortable restriction in her throat, managing to breathe again now she had been freed from his mesmerising presence. Her skin burned from his touch. She raised a hand to her face, covering the spot where his finger had laid its trail of fire. She closed her eyes, scared and confused. If the merest brush of one finger had this effect on her, what on earth would it be like if he really touched her?

No! Her eyes snapped open. No, that was never going to happen. She wouldn't let it happen. She couldn't. Not ever.

CHAPTER FOUR

'Is Nic OK?'

Stifling a sigh, Hannah glanced up from the paperwork she was going through during her lunch-break and noted the concern on Kirsty's face. 'I assume so. Why do you ask?'

'Well, he's just come back from his rounds and he looks odd.'

'What do you mean, odd?'

Kirsty frowned again, glancing down the corridor before closing the door and crossing to stand by the desk. 'I don't know. Kind of… furtive.'

'Furtive?'

'Yes. And now he's shut himself in the treatment room,' the older woman said, clearly puzzled.

'Is anyone else in there with him?'

'Well, no,' Kirsty admitted. 'He just didn't seem himself. I thought you should check.'

Sighing again, Hannah closed her file and put her

sandwich back in its wrapper. 'I'll see what I can find out,' she agreed with reluctance.

Apparently satisfied, Kirsty returned to her own work. Disgruntled, Hannah walked slowly towards the treatment room. The last thing she needed was to be in Nic's presence more than absolutely necessary. She'd managed to avoid him fairly well since their disastrous supper the week before but every time she did see him, she was on tenterhooks, thinking he was going to refer back to their embarrassing conversation at any moment. So far he hadn't, but she wasn't about to push her luck. She had the uncomfortable feeling he was biding his time.

Fortunately, not only had his belongings arrived from Italy at the weekend, keeping him occupied sorting things out in his room, but Allan Pollock had come up with a car. Hannah had scarcely been able to hide her relief. Mobile, Nic had taken on home visits and out-of-hours calls on his own, cutting down the time she had to spend with him.

Now she paused outside the treatment room, wondering what had happened to make Kirsty suspicious. She listened, but there were no sounds from within. Frowning, she hesitated, but as she closed her fingers on the doorhandle, she heard muffled curses from within.

'Come on, *gattino. Lotta*—fight, little one. No, no, *maledizione*! *Non sto lasciandoli morire*! I'm not letting you die.'

Kirsty had been certain no one else was in the treatment room, so who on earth was Nic talking to? Unable to bear another moment of suspense, Hannah quietly opened the door and stepped inside, speechless at the scene that greeted her.

'Nic?'

He looked up, an endearingly guilty look on his face, like a child caught with its hand in the cake tin. 'Hannah!'

'What on earth is going on?' she demanded, finding her voice at last, unable to take her eyes from the minuscule scrap of fur on the treatment table, supported with exquisite gentleness by one of Nic's olive-toned hands.

'I was coming back from calls, *cara*, and there was this sack beside the road. It moved, so I stopped, yes, to look? I found some kittens,' he added, anger and disgust at the cruelty evident in his emotional tone. 'The rest were dead, but this little man, he has a chance.'

Hannah's stomach tightened at the hopeless waste. 'What did you do?'

'He was more dead than alive, frightened and cold

and dehydrated, so I put him inside my jumper, put the sack in the boot and came back here.'

'But—'

He looked up at her, his eyes determined. 'I'm not letting him die, Hannah.'

'No. No, of course not.' She was incredibly touched by his compassion and sensitivity. 'What can I do to help?'

'You're not mad at me?'

His eyes twinkled, drawing a reluctant smile from her. 'I should be, it is a bit unconventional. Goodness knows what anyone would think.'

'It will be our secret. Yes?'

'OK.'

What was it about this man that made her go against her better judgement? She met his gaze and he smiled, a slow, warm, intimate smile that seemed to suck all the breath from her lungs and turn her insides to jelly. Dear God, what was happening to her?

'I put a hot pack to warm. Could you fetch it for me, *cara*?'

Thankful to have something to do, Hannah crossed the room and tested the temperature of the pack to make sure it wasn't too hot. Wrapping it in a towel, she handed it to Nic, who set the little kitten on top.

'Do you think it will be all right?' she asked,

watching as he worked, carefully drying the little scrap and urging it back to life.

'I hope so. But he's very young.'

'What age do you think?'

Nic shrugged. 'About three weeks, maybe four. His eyes are open, but they have not yet changed colour.'

'You seem to know a lot about it. Have you done this before?'

'Sadly, yes.'

Moved by the look of remembered hurt in his eyes, Hannah bent to get a better view of their tiny patient, who stared back myopically and let out a plaintive mew.

'See, he is a fighter!' Nic grinned.

Unexpected tears pricked Hannah's eyes at Nic's obvious care for anything that needed him. He had healing hands, she decided, watching the gentleness with which he touched the kitten. A pale ginger colour, the little animal had a white tip to his skinny tail and an untidy scruff of hair around his scrawny neck, like a mane. Tiny white claws peeped out from the tips of minuscule paws, the pads underneath pink, Hannah noted. She straightened, trying to pull herself together. This was a busy doctor's surgery, not a home for waifs and strays.

'Shona's husband is a vet. He has a practice in

Rigtownbrae, about eight miles away. You're off this afternoon so why don't you take the kitten there and let Alistair look him over and make some suggestions?'

'I will. Thank you.'

'You'll have to get past Kirsty, though. She sent me in here. Said you looked furtive when you came back.'

'Did she?' His dark eyes shone with laughter. 'Maybe I doubted how she would feel if she knew what I was up to.'

'And you knew how I'd react?' she queried, regretting too late that she was stepping on dangerous ground.

His gaze held hers, sending a shiver of fearful awareness down her spine. 'I think I'm coming to know you very well, Hannah,' he replied huskily, unnerving her.

'Then you'll know it's past time I got back to work,' she retorted, stepping away.

'I know that's what you think,' he said with an enigmatic smile, concentrating on wrapping the little kitten up for the journey to the vet. 'I'll see you later.'

Discomfited, Hannah watched him walk away, hearing the oohs and ahs as he paused in Reception to show Kirsty and Jane the kitten, before leaving on his mercy mission.

Back in her consulting room, Hannah disposed of the remains of her sandwich, her appetite having deserted her. All she seemed to be able to think about was Nic and the havoc he was playing with her life and her peace of mind. He had upset everything, disturbing her, pressuring her, questioning her…tempting her. She had started to think of things long forgotten and discarded. Things she had no wish to start up again. Perhaps because she had never met anyone to whom she had been attracted in the past, she had never been tested, never had any cause to question her chosen path. It had been so easy to stick to her decision to focus solely on the career she loved to the exclusion of all else. In a short time Nic had upset her equilibrium and she was frightened where it could lead.

Nic was relaxing in the living room when he heard the front door open and Hannah return home. Funny how he, who had become so scared of putting down any kind of roots in the last two years, thought of this as home after just two weeks. Maybe it was better not to go there. He frowned, tossing his book aside. He glanced up as Hannah hesitated in the doorway, her gaze sweeping round the room.

'Have you cleared up?'

'Hello to you, also.' Nic smiled, amused at her surprise. 'I vacuumed and did a few things. Is that wrong?'

'Not exactly.'

'So?'

She shifted uncomfortably. 'I didn't expect you to be doing chores around the house and cleaning up after me.'

'Why should you clean up after me?' he challenged softly. 'I don't know what kind of men you have lived with in the past, Hannah, but we are not all…what do you call them? Couch potatoes? I certainly do not expect to be waited on.'

He heard her soft intake of breath as she stared at him, clearly uneasy.

'What's wrong?'

'Nothing.'

Her rebuttal was unconvincing. 'Which part of that remark has upset you?' he mused, watching the play of emotions across her face.

'How did you get on with the vet?'

Nic raised an eyebrow at her unsubtle change of subject. He waited a moment, wondering whether to let her get away with it or not, but she looked so anxious he gave in. Again. But only for now. He already had a whole list of interesting things he planned to discuss with her...when the time was right. He had learned, however, not to push her too far too soon.

'Alistair was very helpful.'

'Good.' Relief washed across her face and he knew it wasn't because of the kitten. 'Is he going to find it a new home?'

'Not exactly.'

His evasive statement had Hannah pausing as she turned to leave the room. Her eyes narrowed. 'You've brought him home, haven't you?'

'The vet or the cat?' he teased, earning himself another fiery glare.

'Nic!'

'OK,' he relented. 'Yes, I have. Did you really think I wouldn't?'

'I suppose not. Where is he?'

Nic rose to his feet and walked with her to the kitchen. 'Alistair lent me a kitten pen and I bought some other things we need.'

'We?'

He smiled as her gaze softened when she looked at the kitten asleep in his pen, cuddled up to a soft toy on top of a covered hot-water bottle.

'His name is Wallace.'

'Wallace? After William?'

'No! Did you never hear of Wallace the lion?' he asked, but she shook her head. 'My mama and grandpapa used to read me the comic poem "The Lion and Albert" when I was a child. This little one just looks like a lion, no?'

'Nic, he's nothing like a lion!'

Delighted to hear her laugh, Nic grinned. 'He has a little mane like a lion, no? And he certainly has the fight and courage of one.'

She sobered and glanced at him. 'What about the others?'

'They are buried, *cara*,' he confirmed softly.

Looking sad, she turned back to Wallace. 'It's madness to keep him,' she sighed, looking again at the little ball of fur.

'Don't you ever do mad things now and again?'

'No.'

'Maybe it's time you started.'

She straightened, avoiding his gaze. 'And what is supposed to happen to him when you leave?'

'Wallace can keep you company and look after you for me.'

He could see his words had rattled her, made her back off again, as if things were getting too heavy for her to handle. 'I don't need looking after,' she refuted, her voice cool and distant.

'Don't you?' He watched her knot her fingers together in anxiety. 'And I suppose you don't need company, either?'

Bruised green eyes looked at him. 'Why are you doing this?'

'What do you think I'm doing?'

'I don't know.' She pushed back some wayward strands of hair. 'I—'

Temptation bettered him as a curl of desire licked through his gut. He reached out, ignoring her protesting gasp as he pulled out the pins and watched her hair cascade down around her shoulders.

'Nic?'

'I've wanted to do this since the moment I first met you,' he whispered, running his fingers through the lustrous chestnut thickness. 'You have such beautiful hair, Hannah, you shouldn't hide it.'

Trembling, she pushed his hands away. 'Stop it!'

'Does it upset you that I find you attractive?'

'You can't.' Green eyes widened in shocked alarm. 'You mustn't.'

'Why?'

'Leave me alone, Nic.'

He allowed her retreat, wondering how he was going to break through the barriers she had placed between herself and the rest of the world. What had happened to make her so sad, so alone, so scared? A lost love? He didn't yet know but, despite her protests, her eyes sent out mixed messages and he wasn't going to give up on her.

Wallace mewed plaintively and Nic sighed, gently lifting the warm little body out of the pen, holding him close while he prepared his food. 'Looks like it's just me and you for now, *uomo piccolo.*'

As the days went by, Hannah felt on edge. Nic seemed to be chipping away a bit at a time at her defences, fortifications she had once assured herself were impenetrable. That he had admitted he was attracted to her shocked her to the core. It frightened her but also made her feel an unwanted and alarming tingle of awareness, which confused her even more. She'd given him no encouragement, had tried to be cool and distant from the first. He must have countless women falling over him, so how could he be interested in her?

'You're away with the fairies today, girl!'

The joking admonishment jerked Hannah from her reverie. 'Jimmy, I'm sorry,' she apologised, her cheeks warming.

'Aye, well, I reckon it's not surprising the way you've been working of late,' he stated with concern. 'And you look far too tired. You need a holiday now you have the new locum.'

'I'm fine, Jimmy.'

'Settling in all right, is he?'

'Who?' she fudged, stalling for time.

'The angel doctor.' Jimmy laughed at the look on her face. 'Aye, that's what they're calling him, girl. You did a good job, finding him.'

Hannah busied herself taking Jimmy McCall's blood pressure, disturbed by his words. The angel doctor with the healing touch. Concentrating on her task, she removed her stethoscope and unwound the band from Jimmy's arm. She sat back and looked at him, wrapped in a blanket in his chair by the fire.

'Are your sister and nephew still visiting every week?'

'Aye, lot of fuss the pair of them make. She does like to tidy does Alice. But she makes a good casserole. Not that I can eat much now. What with the family and the home help, plus you and the nurses, I'm not for want of company. And I have the odd surprise guest now and then,' he added, tapping the side of his nose.

Hannah smiled, moved by his spirit. 'So, how are you feeling, really?'

'Oh, you know, not too bad.' The sixty-eight-year-old widower shrugged with a sad smile. 'For a dying man.'

'Don't talk like that, Jimmy.'

'I'm not daft, girl.'

She leaned forward, holding his bony hand, knowing that his cancer was advanced and untreatable, that at best they could keep him comfortable and at home, as he wished, for his last days or weeks. 'Is there anything you need?'

'I've made peace with most people.' He smiled. 'But there is one thing that's bothering me.'

'Can I help?'

'You could,' he allowed mysteriously.

Hannah frowned at him. 'Come on, Jimmy, you're my favourite patient,' she whispered, keeping up their familiar banter, trying to hide her emotions and concern for this man.

'Aye, and you were always my favourite pupil, girl. I mean that. You had so much promise to go with that kind heart of yours. It was a pleasure watching you grow all through your school days. My Jean and I were as proud as anything when you became a doctor. Same as your mum and dad were. You've done us all proud here,' he finished, his voice hoarse, bringing tears to Hannah's eyes.

'Jimmy,' she murmured, but he forestalled her.

'What happened, girl?'

The question surprised her and, tensing, she released his hand and sat back. 'What do you mean?'

'When you came home to us you were so different.' He broke off as a coughing fit caught him and Hannah helped him take a drink of water as it passed. 'Something happened, didn't it, in the city?'

'I just grew up, Jimmy,' she insisted, busying herself packing her things away in her medical bag.

'It was more than that, girl.'

'Jimmy—'

'You never see anyone, have no social life.'

'I'm busy, you know that.'

He regarded her for a moment. 'I hear Sandy Douglas still carries a torch for you.'

'Don't be silly,' she dismissed. 'We went out a couple of times when we were sixteen. There was never anything between us and there never will be.'

'What about the new doctor? He's a nice young man and you get a glint in your eyes when you talk about him!'

'I do not,' she protested in alarm.

'Hannah?'

She rose to her feet, snapping the bag closed and pulling on her coat. 'I know you mean well, Jimmy, but Nic is only here for a few months. Besides, I'm fine as I am. I don't want Sandy Douglas, Nic or anyone else in my life.'

'You asked what you could do for me,' he reminded her, his voice gruff. 'We all love you here in Lochanrig. You are the best of doctors, but you've lost yourself somewhere along the way. That's my last wish, girl, for you to be happy, to bring the old Hannah back.'

Jimmy's words plagued her as she drove back to the surgery, her eyes blurred. At least it was Saturday lunchtime and everyone would have gone, she thought, blinking away fresh tears. Her relief was short-lived and she groaned when she saw Nic's car in the parking space next to hers. This was all she needed, now of all times. Flipping down the sun visor, she checked her appearance in the mirror, wiping away any signs of her tears.

She unlocked the surgery door and walked in, planning to head quietly to her consulting room undetected, but Nic was standing behind the reception desk, checking a patient's notes and talking on the phone. He looked up, the beginnings of a smile dying on his face as he looked at her.

Oh, God! How could she have imagined he wouldn't notice? Hannah felt nervous tension coil through her. Dragging her gaze away, she headed for her room, hearing him return his attention to his telephone conversation.

'Sorry,' he said to the caller. 'I'm still here. Paracetamol and plenty of water and fruit juice to drink. That's right. Call again if you are worried, yes?'

She barely had time to set her bag down and take off her coat before there was a tap on her door and Nic came in.

'Hannah?'

'Yes?' she said, concentrating far more than necessary on the task of hanging up her coat.

'What's wrong?'

She closed her eyes. His voice was closer. Too close. 'Nothing,' she refuted as lightly as she could. She tried to step away, but his hand on her arm made her freeze.

'Why do you do that?' he demanded, sounding frustrated, turning her to face him. 'Why do you deny your own hurt?'

'I don't.'

'You do it all the time,' he corrected her, his voice more gentle, concern in his compelling dark eyes.

Alarmed, she freed her arm from his hold, taking a step back, uncomfortable at the physical contact. 'I'm fine. I was just…concerned about a patient.' Nic stood there, arms folded across his chest, blocking her retreat. 'I've been out to see Jimmy McCall.'

'We've met.'

'Have you?' She glanced up at him in surprise. 'I didn't know that.'

'You've known him a long time.'

It was a statement, not a question, and Hannah nodded, fighting for control, pushing the memories of Jimmy's last words away. 'All my life. I hate that I can't do anything more for him,' she admitted, cursing the wobble in her voice.

'You're allowed to care, *innamorata*, to hurt, to be human.'

She sucked in a breath and bit her lip, unable to say anything, desperate not to cry in front of him.

'You give everything to others but never take anything for yourself,' he whispered, his hands taking her reluctant ones in his. 'It's not a crime to need someone, to let someone help you.'

'Nic…'

He let go of her hands and opened his arms. 'A hug, yes?'

She couldn't. He waited patiently, unthreatening, letting her make up her mind. Confused, she met his dark gaze, seeing nothing but kindness. She didn't do this sort of thing, shouldn't even be tempted, but something about Nic made her act out of character. A tiny step nearer him and she hesitated, uncertain. He took a step to meet her, his arms gently closing round her.

'Nic, I—'

Her whispered words were muffled against the hard wall of his chest and she held herself stiffly in his arms, her hands lifting to his sides, clenching in the fabric of his jacket, unsure whether she was trying to push him away or hold him close—too scared to find out.

'Relax,' he soothed, one hand moving lightly on her back. 'You don't like to be hugged?'

Fresh tears pricked her eyes as she shook her head. 'No,' she whispered. She hated being touched at all. It made her skin crawl when she thought about... With a desperate effort she pushed the unwanted memories away, but the remembered panic had made her tense and she could feel a tremor run through her.

'Everything's OK, *cara.*'

Nic's soft reassurances confused her and she wondered how she could feel so scared and so safe at the same time. Warmth seemed to permeate her whole body from the top of her head to the tips of her toes, and every time she breathed in she absorbed Nic's scent, his sandalwood aftershave mixed with something elementally him.

She had no idea how long they stood there, but when Nic finally eased away, she looked up at him in confusion, alarmed at the way his eyes darkened, his gaze intent as he stared back at her. When he bent his head so that his lips brushed hers with gentle softness, Hannah thought she would expire with shock. She was desperate to pull away but she couldn't move, held captive by his sheer magnetism. The caress was almost chaste, yet held the promise— or the threat—of so much more. The thought permeated and she jerked her head back from him.

A small smile played around his mouth as he stepped back a pace, taking hold of her hands again. 'Come on, we're getting out of here.'

'What?'

'It's a free Saturday afternoon for us both. We're going to have some fun.'

Hannah stared at him. 'Fun?'

'Have you not heard of it?' he teased.

'Of course, but—'

'Are you always so controlled?'

'Aren't we all?'

'I don't feel in control when I'm with you,' he confided, shocking her. 'Not at all.'

'Nic—'

'It's scary but exciting.'

She didn't want to think about these things, didn't want to listen to him. 'Don't.'

'We make a deal. Come with me now, or…'

'Or?' she whispered as he paused, hardly daring to hear the answer as she saw the intent expression in his eyes.

'Or I kiss you again—properly this time.'

Renewed panic set in and she looked back at him, wide-eyed. 'I'll get my coat and bag.'

Laughing, Nic let go of her hands and she tried to regroup as she picked up her things and followed him out of the surgery.

'Where are we going?'

'You'll see. I'll meet you back at the house.'

Puzzled, Hannah followed him home. 'Nic—'

'Go and change,' he instructed her as they faced each other in the hall. 'Jeans, jumper, boots, gloves and something warm, OK?'

'But—'

'Go, or I might forget our deal!'

Filled with nervous apprehension, Hannah met him back downstairs ten minutes later to discover he had also changed and was seeing to Wallace, settling the little kitten back in his pen. He turned and smiled, nodding his approval of her outfit as she pulled on a thick jacket. Taking her hesitant hand in his, he led her out of the house.

'No way!' she protested when she realised he was heading towards his motorbike.

'Have you been on one?'

'Of course not! And I'm not going to now.'

He set two helmets on the seat and faced her. 'Don't you ever take risks? Feel alive?'

'No.'

'You do now.'

Ignoring her mumbled protests, he helped her on with a helmet, double-checking that it fitted. Then made sure her gloves were on and she was well buttoned up for the cold before he swung onto the bike with effortless ease and started the engine. As it throbbed in the stillness of the afternoon, Nic gave her a few instructions.

'Sit up close to me. You can either hold the bar behind you, or you can hold me,' he added with a smile, daring her, tempting her. 'Whichever you find more comfortable. Watch what I'm doing and how I lean. Move gently with me, and keep your feet on the pegs. OK?'

Hannah stared at him. 'Nic…?'

'Trust me, *innamorata*.'

He held his hand out to her and waited. She really didn't want to do this but something about Nic made her behave in the most foolish of ways. Placing her hand in his, she allowed him to steady her as she climbed on behind him. Closing her eyes as Nic pulled on his own helmet and gloves, Hannah clasped the little handle thing behind her as instructed and held on. He kicked up the rest and eased slowly down the drive.

It was a beautiful late October day, the sun low in the sky, the trees and hedgerows turning golden browns and russet reds. Her fear subsiding, Hannah found herself relaxing, although she didn't feel so comfortable holding onto the grip behind her seat. When they stopped at a crossroad, he glanced back to see if she was OK. Hesitantly she released her hold and forced herself to inch forward and slide her arms around his waist. Despite it being windy and cold in the breeze from the bike, she found she was enjoying herself. As Nic headed up into the hills, her confidence in him was growing, he was in charge and would keep her safe.

They stopped a few times to absorb the views of hillsides and hidden lochs, the heather almost over now but the bracken turning. The southern uplands were so beautiful that she sighed, flipping up her visor to breathe in the crisp autumn air. When they stopped by St Mary's Loch, she wished she had the free time to come out here more often, to lose herself in the tranquil, unpopulated remoteness of her home landscape. They moved on again, stopping for Nic to see the Grey Mare's Tail waterfall before heading on towards the pretty town of Moffat. The landscape was incredible, and she felt more at ease, both on the bike and with Nic. It was the most exhilarating afternoon of her life! She grinned, surprising herself, sorry when they headed back towards Lochanrig and Nic finally drew the bike to a halt outside the house.

Hannah released her hold on him, pulling off her gloves to fumble with the strap of her helmet, her nerves returning as Nic's hands moved to help her, his fingers brushing against hers. She slid off the bike, her legs shaky, and handed him the helmet.

His dark gaze slid over her. 'OK?'

Hannah nodded, feeling shy and uneasy again.

'Did you enjoy it?' he asked with a smile, stepping off the bike.

'Yes,' she was forced to admit. 'Thank you.'

Nic took her hand, silken lashes fanning his cheeks as he closed his eyes and pressed a kiss to her palm, making her skin tingle. His eyes opened, warm and disturbing, his voice husky with promise. 'Any time, Hannah. Any time.'

Trembling, she watched as Nic walked away from her towards the house, very much afraid that his promise offered her more than just another trip on his bike.

CHAPTER FIVE

THE crisp, sunny days of October were replaced with rain and wind as November arrived. Nothing else had happened between Nic and herself since the ride on his bike, but Hannah felt as if she was living in a tinderbox that would flare up at the slightest provocation. She felt more jumpy than ever, conscious of Nic's dark gaze on her whenever they were together, knowing that he watched her and that he saw too much. Pushing her concerns away, Hannah concentrated on her task.

'You must get Gavin to Casualty now, Mrs Miller,' she stressed, making sure the boy who had tumbled from his bike was as comfortable as possible. 'I'm sure it is just a simple fracture but it will need an X-ray and cast. And I imagine they will check to make sure he didn't knock his head. Do you need me to call an ambulance for you?'

'No, Doctor, don't you worry none. My husband's on his way home from work and he'll drive us down.'

'All right. Just let me know if there is anything I can do.'

'Long-term sedation would be appealing,' she admitted with a harassed smile. 'You need eyes in the back of your head with this boy.'

Smiling back, Hannah packed her bag and ruffled young Gavin's blond curls. 'Take care, young man.'

'Thanks for coming, Doctor,' Mrs Miller sighed, seeing her out.

'No problem.'

Glancing at her watch and seeing how late she was, having had this emergency call added at the end of her home visits, Hannah drove back to the surgery.

'I'm glad you're here,' Jane greeted her.

'What's wrong?'

'Nic. He's not very well. Kirsty and Morag are in his room trying to persuade him to go home.'

More concerned than she wanted to admit, Hannah left the patient notes with Jane to file away and walked along to Nic's consulting room.

'Ah, Hannah.' Kirsty smiled grimly, hands on hips, a determined glint in her eye. 'Perhaps you can talk some sense into the man.'

Morag moved from her place beside Nic and gestured Hannah forward. 'I'll go and get my car so I can run him home and get him settled.'

'You're all fussing about nothing,' Nic protested, but he didn't sound his usual energetic and mischievous self.

'I'll start moving appointments,' Kirsty insisted firmly, bustling from the room.

Hannah looked at Nic for a moment, seeing the pallor beneath the unnatural flush on his cheeks, the slightly glazed look in his eyes. She walked round the desk, a frown on her face.

'How are you feeling?' she asked him.

'I probably just ate something that disagreed with me.'

'You look funny.'

'Is that a professional medical term?' he queried, his eyes crinkling at the corners as he managed a weak smile, before leaning back in the chair with a smothered groan, his eyes closing.

'I'm serious, Nic.' The man was impossible. She laid her hand on his forehead. 'You're burning up! This is silly. You've obviously picked up some bug or other. Let Morag give you a lift home and get some rest. You are not to come back in today, that's an order. I can manage surgery and you can ring down if you need anything. We'll see how things are tomorrow.'

'OK.' He gave in with obvious reluctance. '*Dio*, you can be bossy, Dr Frost.'

'Just remember it and do as you're told,' she chided, noting how shaky he was when he got to his feet.

Concerned, she walked with him to Reception and allowed Morag to take over as she rushed into mother-hen mode and ushered Nic out to her car. 'Don't worry, I'll see he has fluids to hand and is warm,' the kindly nurse reassured Hannah.

It was late by the time Hannah was free to go back to the house, surgery having overrun because she had taken Nic's patients as well as her own. She let herself into the house, her concern increasing when she found him flaked out on the settee, where Morag had left him, looking decidedly peaky. She'd told the silly man he wasn't well. Not that it gave her any satisfaction to be proved right.

'Nic?' Hannah frowned, seeing how shivery he was, his skin clammy to the touch. 'Come on, let's get you up to bed. You're going to have to help me.'

He mumbled something but did as she told him, although it took a ridiculous amount of time before he was safely up the stairs and they were edging along to his room. Once there, he tumbled rather unceremoniously onto the bed, and Hannah found herself sprawled haphazardly beside him, her arm wedged underneath his shoulders. She freed herself and sat up, breathless from the effort.

'Nic, can you get undressed?'

He groaned, eyes closed, breathing laboured. It seemed the last of his energy had been sapped reaching his room, so she steeled herself to do the job, trying not to be rough but having a bit of a struggle as he was too weak and out of it to be of much help. She finally managed to peel off his jumper, shoes and socks, then hesitated, a lump in her throat, before her fingers fumbled with the belt and fastening of his trousers.

The task done, she fetched an extra sheet and blankets and covered him with them before putting the duvet back on top, telling herself she really hadn't been unprofessional and had not allowed herself any lingering appraisal of his well-defined torso, with its dusting of dark hair arrowing down his abdomen, his intriguing muscles and textures, olive-toned skin and long legs. Uncomfortable, she checked his temperature, concerned how his fever was raging, and went to get her medical bag and some fluids for him.

When he was sleeping fitfully, she hurried around, doing the chores, seeing to Wallace and locking up, then made herself a sandwich and coffee and took them back to Nic's room, along with something to read. Feeling pooped herself, she settled down in a cosy chair for her vigil.

'Wally, your food smells revolting,' Hannah complained two days later, shaking her head as the kitten received it joyfully and then seemed to get more all over himself than he ate, each little foot paddling in the shallow bowl.

Lifting him out when he had finished, she gently wiped him over, a smile curving her mouth as she admitted how cute he was. 'At least you're an easier patient to look after than your master,' she murmured, a frown replacing her smile.

Nic's fever and sickness had run for over twenty-four hours and either Debbie, Shona or Morag had covered for her during the day, checking on him while she herself had managed the surgery and house calls.

'There you go, little man,' she murmured to Wallace, unconsciously mirroring Nic's nickname for the kitten as she settled him back in his pen. 'I'd better go and check on him, see if he's ready for some supper.'

She was going mad now, talking to a cat. Smiling, she went up the stairs and peeped round Nic's door, relieved the nurses had managed to persuade him into pyjama bottoms and a T-shirt. At least he'd been too ill to know anything when she'd had to care for him herself that first night, but now he was on the mend and getting more difficult, as well as bored with staying in bed.

'How are you feeling?'

'Better, but pathetically weak,' he allowed, shifting further up in the bed and propping himself on the pillows.

Hannah's gaze skittered away from him. He looked like a rogue with a couple of days' stubble darkening his jaw. As ever her insides tied them-selves into knots when she was anywhere near him.

'Do you feel like anything to eat?' she asked now, fussing with the bed clothes. 'I was going to make omelettes.'

'That sounds great. I'll come down.'

'Not until tomorrow, you won't.'

She jumped when his fingers curled round her wrist. 'Your bedside manner could do with some working on, Dr Frost. You can be a hard woman,' he teased.

'As I remember it, you are supposed to be here as an extra doctor, not an extra patient,' she pointed out, hoping to distract attention from the way her pulse had started racing from his touch.

'I'm sorry about that, *cara*,' he apologised, immediately contrite. His gaze scanned her face. 'You look tired. Give me tomorrow to recover and I'll be back at work on Monday.'

'Don't worry about it.'

'Hannah—'

She managed to free her arm and stepped out of reach. 'I'll bring your omelette up shortly.'

'Bring yours, too, I'd enjoy your company.'

Hannah had no intention whatsoever of sitting on his bed, eating her supper! The sooner he was up and about again, the better.

'So tell me all the news,' Nic suggested a while later as they finished their omelettes and Hannah sat awkwardly on his bed, wondering how she had ended up in this situation after all.

She busied herself peeling and coring an apple to share with him. 'There hasn't been anything very exciting happening—except the little boy who managed to get his fingers stuck in his toy train!'

'You're kidding?' He laughed, dropping weakly back against the pillows.

'Nope.' Her stomach turned over just looking at him. 'His fingers had swollen so much we had to send him down to Casualty. Come on, now, you get some rest.'

'I'm fine,' he protested.

Hannah couldn't help but smile. 'Sure you are. That's why you've had the undivided attention of three nurses and a doctor for the last forty-eight hours, mopping your fevered brow!'

'I'll have to remember your expert diagnosis, *innamorata*,' he joked, raising his eyebrows, a smile curving that far too tempting mouth. 'What was it again? "You look funny"?'

'At the moment you look like a pirate,' she quipped sarcastically.

Nic ran a hand over his stubbled jaw, drawing her attention shamefully to his rakish good looks. 'I'll be up tomorrow and restored to respectability.'

'Just take things easy this time. Remember you nearly fell over when you tried that this morning.' Her gaze met his for another long, breath-stealing moment, then she gathered up the plates. 'I've got paperwork to do, so I'll leave you some things to read if you're bored, but try and get some more sleep. And before you ask for the hundredth time, Wallace is fine.'

'Thank you.'

'It's OK. Now, do as you're told!'

'Like I said, you're a hard woman, Dr Frost.' His smile warmed her from the inside out. 'I'll be all right, you know, if you want to join the others for the firework party this evening.'

The words caught her unawares and she froze, fumbling the plates. 'I don't want to,' she snapped, hearing the tension in her voice.

'Hannah?'

Damn him! She saw the puzzled concern at her change of mood but could do nothing to alter it. She hated November the fifth. It had happened on Bonfire Night, with the sky ablaze and the air filled with the sound of rockets and laughter and... Fighting back the memories, she dragged her gaze from Nic's.

'I don't like fireworks. Rest now,' she mumbled, hurrying from his room.

Hannah was about to slip into bed about three hours later when she hesitated. Had Nic called her? He'd been sleeping peacefully when she had checked him a while ago. Frowning, she pulled her robe on over her pyjamas, knotting it round her waist as she padded barefoot down the landing, her concern growing as she heard Nic shouting out in distress.

Rushing into his room, she stopped, realising he was dreaming, tossing to and fro on the bed, talking in his native language, his words urgent and anguished. What demons tortured his sleep? Concerned, Hannah crossed to the bed and switched on the side light.

'Nic.' She gave him a gentle shake, repeating it more strongly as he failed to stir. 'Nic! Wake up.'

Finally her efforts had an effect and he woke with a start, staring at her in confusion, the pain in his eyes tugging at her heart.

'What happened?' he queried, clearly trying to make sense of where he was and why she was there.

'You were having a bad dream.'

'I'm sorry I disturbed you.'

Hannah shook her head, feeling at a loss, moved by the despair in his voice. 'You were talking, calling for someone, more than one person.'

'Lorenzo,' he breathed, his eyes closing.

'Yes.' Hannah bit her lip, curious despite herself but hating to intrude. 'And Federica, is it?'

His eyes opened again, reflecting some terrible inner pain. 'Federica, *sì.*' He draped an arm across his face as if trying to block out the memories, the hurt.

'Do you want to tell me about it?'

'The region of Italy I called home is prone to earthquakes,' he told her after long moments of silence, his voice raw. 'Just over two years ago we were hit by a big one. I was at the hospital some miles away. Everyone at home was lost. My parents, my elder brother, Lorenzo, his wife…'

'Federica?' she supplied when he paused.

'No, Sofia was Lorenzo's wife. Federica was my fiancée.'

Tears pricked Hannah's eyes and she didn't want to examine the rush of mixed emotions that assailed her at the horrible news, or at knowing Nic had loved this unknown woman, Federica.

'Nic, I'm so sorry.'

Without thinking, she sat on the edge of the bed, holding his hand in hers, aware of its strength and its gentleness and its warmth.

'I've never talked about this before.'

'Maybe it's a good thing you do now, then,' she prompted softly.

His dark gaze held hers captive. 'Do as you say and not as you do, is that right, *cara*?'

'I don't know what you mean.'

'Oh, I think you do. So we make a deal, yes?' he suggested, the fingers of the hand she held twining sinuously and disturbingly with hers, preventing her withdrawal. 'I tell you my secrets, you tell me yours. We share each other's pain.'

Alarmed, she sought an escape route. 'Nic, I—'

At that moment a firework went off at a neighbouring house and Hannah jumped out of her skin, a startled cry drawn from her.

Feeling her tremble with fear as more loud bangs sounded, Nic looked at her pale face and haunted eyes. 'You really are frightened of fireworks, aren't you?'

'Did you think I was making it up?'

'No, but…' He just wasn't sure where it fitted in with the rest of the jigsaw puzzle he was trying to piece together about her. 'Come here.'

Holding her hand, knowing she would bolt given half the chance, Nic steered her round to the other side of the bed. He flipped up the duvet only, so that the extra sheet and blanket he'd been using while ill remained between them, and encouraged her to sit down.

'I don't think this is a good idea,' she resisted.

'You're quite safe, Hannah.'

He could feel her tension and her fear as he gently encouraged her down with him, folding the duvet back over her rigid form. Lying on their sides, with her back towards him, her head was pillowed on his arm, his hand still holding hers. With his free hand, he brushed some of the loose strands of hair back from her face, revelling in being able to touch it. He closed his eyes, breathing in the scent of her shampoo mixed with the vanilla fragrance of her perfume, warm, pure and arousing.

A distant volley of fireworks exploded and he felt the shiver run through her. He stroked her hair, urging her to relax.

'I o-ought to go and check W-Wallace. He might be f-frightened.'

'He'll be fine,' Nic soothed, knowing the kitten was safe and protected. It was her fear that concerned him. 'Hannah—'

'Tell me about your family,' she whispered.

And so he did, finding that although the past still haunted him, he could talk about his parents, his brother and sister-in-law, even Federica, with warmth and love and humour, and that the pain, though always there, had lost its power to destroy him.

'Had you and Federica been together long?'

'Five years, nearly to the day." He sighed, remembering the woman with whom he had expected to spend the rest of his life. 'We had everything planned, how many children we would have, everything.'

'You wanted a family?'

Nic frowned, hearing the stiffness in Hannah's voice. 'Yes, of course. I'm Italian!' But she didn't laugh as he had meant her to, and his frown deepened.

'So what happened?' she asked after a long silence.

'One day we all breakfasted together, happy, making plans for the weekend. A few hours later, they were all gone, in the blink of an eye.' He hesitated, finding the words difficult. 'And I was not there.'

'It wasn't your fault.'

'I should have been with them when they needed me.'

'So you could have died as well?' she protested. 'Who would that have helped?'

Her stark words made him pause. 'Perhaps it would have helped me, *cara*,' he finally whispered, his voice choked with anguish. 'Then I would not have been the only one left to identify the broken bodies of my parents, my fiancée, my brother and sister-in-law.'

He let go of her hand as she wriggled round to face him, gold-flecked green eyes shadowed in the pale glow from the lamp, reflecting her sorrow and her compassion. Tentatively, as if fighting some inner struggle, she reached out a hand and softly touched his face.

'It must have been terrible to cope with that alone.'

Nic just nodded, affected by the feel of her fingers on his skin. She was so close. If he moved a few inches he could kiss her and—

'Is that why you've travelled around so much the last couple of years?'

Her question snapped him back to his senses. 'Yes. I don't do commitment, I don't put down roots. Not any more.'

His loss had devastated him, left him homeless, searching for something unknown yet never seeming to belong. Now, for the first time in a long while, he felt settled. As much as he loved his own country, there was something captivating about this place and these people that made him feel…what? He frowned, recognising the danger of his thoughts.

'Nic?'

'There seemed nothing left for me. It was all too painful,' he explained. 'I needed to get away, to come to terms with it, to see if I could go on.'

'And you can. You have.'

'Yes, but not without the guilt that I am alive and they are not.'

Her hand retreated and she tipped her head back to look at him. 'Would any of them have wanted you to die?'

'No, of course not,' he responded in shock.

'And had you been there when it happened and any of them had been elsewhere, safe, would you have wanted them back with you, to die with you?'

'*Dio!*' The shock turned to a slow-burning anger. 'What do you think of me?'

'Nic, I'm trying to make you see that as you wouldn't have wanted any of them to die with you, neither would they have wanted you to die. Knowing that you were away, safe, probably gave them huge comfort. Not all was lost.'

He ran a hand through his hair in agitation, struggling with himself, mulling over what she had said, but the rare flash of anger was gone.

'You have nothing to feel guilty for, Nic, it was the cruelty of fate. The same for my mother being in the wrong place at the wrong time. It's not your fault you are alive. Instead, you are giving of yourself to help others, to heal them.'

He was silent for a long time but he could almost feel a new calmness seep into him.

'Thank you, *innamorata*.'

As if she heard something new in his voice, he saw alarm flicker in her eyes and she smiled dismissively, inching further away, her gaze sliding from his.

'Hannah…'

She stopped wriggling and met his gaze with obvious reluctance. 'What?'

'One day—soon—I'm going to help you heal.'

His fingers at her wrist felt the rapid flicker of her pulse and he watched as she raised her free hand unconsciously to her throat in a protective, shielding gesture. 'I'm fine,' she finally responded, but her voice was hoarse with discomfort.

Dio, she was beautiful. Complex, mysterious and enigmatic, she sent out jumbled signals, but she excited him more than any other woman had ever done—even Federica, he realised with a stab of guilt at his disloyalty. Watching the play of emotions in Hannah's eyes, he allowed the fingers of one hand to trace the line of freckles across her face. He heard the cadence of her breathing change and her lashes drifted shut, only to snap open again when he brushed the pad of his thumb across her lips.

'Nic?' she whispered, sounding uncertain and scared.

'Shush.'

His thumb under her chin, he bent his head with infinite care and touched his mouth to hers. Slowly, slowly, he told himself, fighting the rush of desire that swept through him. Don't mess this up.

The tip of his tongue teased along the line of her lips and she gasped, trembling. 'D-don't…'

'I have to,' he whispered back.

A second later she sighed, the sweetness of her breath mingling with his own as her lips parted to the pressure of his.

He had longed for this. Sinking his fingers into the

hair at her nape, he slowly deepened the kiss, coaxing her through her hesitancy and into willing participation, groaning at the tentative exploration as her own tongue glided with his. She tasted exquisite, fresh and pure, and he knew right away he would never tire of kissing her, that he wanted so much more... Nic sensed the moment when Hannah's response changed and panic set in. Then she was pushing against him with a whimper of distress and he forced himself to retreat, pulling back at once.

'It's OK,' he soothed, giving her some space, gently stroking her face. 'What is it that scares you so much?'

She shook her head, withdrawing further, clearly determined to keep her secrets. He let her turn over again, with her back to him, knowing she really wanted to leave.

'Stay,' he urged softly, holding his breath for what seemed an age as she hesitated, deliberating the wisdom of his request.

As she gradually began to relax again, his breath sighed out in relief. He slipped an arm round her, careful to make sure she didn't feel trapped. She wriggled around for a moment, getting comfortable, and he groaned, anything but relaxed when he was so hopelessly aroused. Maybe this hadn't been such a good idea!

'Are you in pain?' she asked with concern.

'Yes.' His smile was rueful as he shifted in the bed, trying to make his problem less obvious. 'But not in the way you are thinking.'

'I don't understand.'

'No, and, believe me, you wouldn't want to!'

'But—'

'Go to sleep, *cara*.'

Nic lay awake for a long time, savouring the feel of her in his arms. He had no illusions that she would still be there in the morning, but for now he could pretend she was his. It nearly killed him not to kiss her, to touch her, to make love to her, but he knew he couldn't. Not yet. For whatever reason, this was as far as she could go for now. He had to be patient, take things slowly.

As he lay listening to her breathing, he thought back to their kiss, a frown on his face. She had seemed uncertain, almost inexperienced. Maybe she was just rusty, out of practice—like him. He smiled into the darkness. If he had his way, they would enjoy plenty of practice in the weeks ahead. All he had to do was persuade Hannah it was what she wanted, too.

CHAPTER SIX

'Hı.'

Hannah glanced up as Nic stepped inside her consulting room, her heart contracting, as it always seemed to, just at the sight of him. 'Hi,' she managed in reply.

He approached the desk with lazy strides. 'I thought you'd like to see this, it's just arrived.'

'What is it?'

She took the postcard he held out to her, a smile spreading across her face as she realised it was from Joanne McStay, the carer they had been so worried about. She had taken their advice for some respite care and this was the result, a glowing account of her two-week holiday in Greece.

'It's great, no?'

'Amazing!' Hannah looked up, her gaze clashing with his, one look at those slumberous dark eyes setting her pulse racing again. 'She sounds happy.'

'Let's hope we can keep her that way when she comes home.'

Nic perched on the corner of her desk, the action tightening the fabric of his dark grey trousers over the muscled length of his thigh.

'Absolutely.'

Hannah cleared her throat, dragging her gaze away. Whatever was wrong with her lately? She couldn't even seem to form a coherent sentence any more. He'd only kissed her, for goodness' sake! Two weeks ago. So why did she think she could still taste him? She sighed, her tongue running over her lips. A faint indrawn breath alerted her and she glanced up, finding his gaze fixed on her mouth, his eyes sultry. Hannah froze. Nothing had happened since that night and yet every look, every innocuous touch seemed more heated, more charged than before.

'There you are, Nic,' Kirsty announced, bustling into the room, seemingly oblivious of the tension that, to Hannah, crackled in the air. 'Mr Maxwell is on the phone, he'd like a word with you about his test results. I've left his notes on your desk.'

'Of course. Thank you, Kirsty,' he responded, although his gaze never left Hannah's face.

'Right you are. Hannah, your first appointment is here.'

'OK.'

Kirsty bustled out again as Nic slowly rose from the desk. 'I'll see you later.' He smiled, his voice more throaty than usual.

'Yes, I expect so,' she agreed, aiming for a nonchalance she was far from feeling. 'Thanks for the card.'

'No problem.'

Hannah sank back into her chair as the door closed behind him, her hands clenching on the arms. Dear God, this had to stop. Compassion for the pain of his loss had overwhelmed both her common sense and her fear of intimacy, so much so she had acted completely out of character. And look where it had led her. Into his arms. She closed her eyes, remembering the texture of his stubbled jaw under her hand, the exciting rasp of it across her skin as he'd kissed her. Heat and anxiety curled inside her in equal measure. She'd never felt anything like this before. Had never been kissed like that before, either, with a combination of such exquisite tenderness and fiery sensuality. When she had been sure Nic had fallen asleep, she had slid from his bed and returned to her room, shaken and confused. And strangely bereft. A feeling that had stayed with her, unnerving, distracting.

Nic had confided in her about the terrible loss of

his family and his fiancée, the tragedy that now drove him from place to place. It sounded as if his heart had been buried with his fiancée, that no one would fill the hole she had left in his life. She knew Nic wanted her to share her secrets with him in return, but she couldn't. She had never told anyone. It had been years since she had even given the events any conscious thought, she realised now. And yet they governed her existence. Back here, in the place she loved, she had found her niche. She felt safe and comfortable and controlled. At least she had, until Nic had arrived and started to upset everything. Now all those bad memories were flowing back to the surface, unsettling her.

For the last two weeks she had tried to avoid him as much as possible, but it wasn't easy, especially at home. He made her feel vulnerable and out of control. She had to remember that she was just a project to him. Another Wallace. Something he thought he could heal while he was there. Then he would be gone and he'd forget all about her. She couldn't allow things to get out of hand, no matter the temptation, because there was no doubt Nic would go and she would be left putting the pieces of her life back together. Again.

'Hannah?'

Her intercom buzzed, making her jump. She sat forward and pressed the button. 'Yes?'

'Is something wrong?' Kirsty asked impatiently, clearly bemused at the delay. 'Are you ready for your patients now?'

'I'm sorry. Of course. Send the first one in.'

Taking the notes from her tray, Hannah drew in a deep breath, endeavouring to put thoughts of Nic, and her past, from her mind and concentrate on her morning list.

It was a long surgery. Everyone seemed to have fiddly or difficult problems, and Hannah was thankful when she showed her last patient out. She was anticipating a reviving cup of coffee when Kirsty appeared at the door, another set of notes in her hand.

'Can you see one more?'

'Of course,' Hannah sighed, smothering a yawn. 'Who is it?'

'Sally, the barmaid from the Furry Ferret,' she sniffed with disapproval, making Hannah smile, both at her tone and the use of the jocular nickname for the local inn.

'What's the problem?'

'She's asking to see Nic but he's already out on calls. Not that I'd let the floosie loose on him. They call her The Piranha, you know.'

'Kirsty!'

The plain-speaking woman sniffed again. 'It's no secret around the village that Sally has set her sights on our new doctor, not that I can see him being remotely interested in *her*! Still, I'm not having her harassing him for irrelevant appointments.'

'Send her in, then,' Hannah requested, taking the notes Kirsty handed her.

She disapproved of gossip, but the news that someone was interested in Nic on a personal level left her feeling distinctly uncomfortable. She frowned as the young woman in question tottered into the room wearing a very low-cut top, a skirt that was so short it was nearly a belt and impossibly high heels.

Hannah smothered a rush of uncharacteristic annoyance and, offering a cool smile, gestured for the young woman to sit down. 'What can I do for you today, Sally?'

'I had been hoping to see Dr di Angelis.' She pouted prettily, tossing bleached blonde curls over her shoulder.

'I'm afraid he's out at the moment. Can I help?'

Disappointment evident, Sally used a long, scarlet-painted nail to sweep her fringe from her heavily mascara'd blue eyes. 'I suppose so. There are a couple of things now I am here.'

'Of course,' Hannah allowed stiffly. 'The first?'

'My eczema is flaring up again. I wonder if there is something different I could try?' she asked, pointing to the reddened patches on her arms, some of which looked inflamed and crusty.

Hannah studied her notes, seeing she had been using Betnovate cream for some while. 'Do you have any patches elsewhere?'

'I sometimes have it behind the knees, but not at the moment.' She grimaced, wrinkling her pert little nose. 'Not very attractive, is it?'

'It can be very unpleasant. You find the Betnovate isn't working for you?'

'Not really.'

Having examined Sally's arms, Hannah tapped out a prescription request on her keyboard and turned to Sally while it printed. 'I'll give you some Dermovate ointment but make sure you use it sparingly and only once a day. You should find it more efficient than the cream you've been using,' she added, signing the prescription and handing it across.

'Thank you, Dr Frost.'

'You might also find it helps to use a cream like E45 or Diprobase to avoid irritating the skin.'

'I'll try that, thanks.'

'Good.' Hannah forced another cool smile. 'Was there something else you wanted to discuss, Sally?'

'Oh, yes, silly me!' She smirked with a tinkly giggle.

Hannah hid her irritation by looking over her notes again. 'How else can I help?' she prompted.

'Birth control.'

'Right.' Hannah felt her jaw tighten involuntarily. 'I see you were taking the Pill until recently?'

'I was, but I stopped them for a while. Now I want to start again. Just in case I get lucky!'

This time Hannah couldn't force a smile as Sally giggled suggestively. 'And did you have any problems taking them before, Sally?'

'No, none at all.'

'I'll just check your blood pressure, if I may.'

Hannah concentrated on her task, not wanting to consider with whom Sally was hoping to 'get lucky'. Something hot and insidious curled inside her. Something that felt suspiciously like jealousy. Nonsense, she berated herself. She unsnapped the cuff and hooked her stethoscope round her neck.

'That's fine,' she confirmed to Sally, writing down the blood-pressure figures in her notes. 'I'll give you a new prescription for the same brand, all right? Come and see me again if you have any problems with them.'

'Thanks.'

Hannah handed over the second prescription, eager for this tortuous consultation to be over, but the attractive blonde still lingered.

'Was there something else, Sally?'

'I wondered... Is the new doctor staying long?'

'Just temporarily,' Hannah said, barely keeping the snap from her voice.

'That's a shame. He's the dishiest man we've had round here in ages! He comes into the pub sometimes with his walking friends,' Sally confided. 'He's always so friendly.'

Hannah gritted her teeth and rose to her feet. 'Is he really?'

Nic occasionally went out in the evenings, she knew not where, but she did know he enjoyed hill walking and mountain biking at the weekends when he wasn't on call. Not that it was any of her business what he did. Or with whom he did it. She frowned. He had clearly been accepted into village life very rapidly, she thought sourly, not quite sure why she was feeling so grumpy and out of sorts.

'Well, thanks,' the girl murmured, reluctantly rising, too. 'Is Dr di Angelis, you know, attached?'

'I really have no idea, Sally. Now, I'm afraid you'll have to excuse me as I'm running late.'

She barely resisted slamming the door as Sally retreated towards Reception in those ridiculous shoes. Serve her right if she ended up in A and E with a broken ankle, Hannah fumed. She wrote up her notes and closed the file with a thud. Stuffing the patient files back in the tray with more force than necessary, she caused the whole lot to shoot off the edge of the desk and spill across the floor. Her temper stoked, Hannah started to retrieve them, resisting the childish temptation to kick the empty plastic tray across the room.

'Bloody woman! Anyone would think I was running a bloody dating service, not a doctor's surgery!'

'Can I help?'

Hannah spun round in shock at the sound of Nic's amused query from the doorway. Bloody man! This was all his fault, anyway. She slammed the tray back on the desk and rammed the notes inside.

'I thought you were out on calls?' she snapped at him.

'I was,' he agreed equably. 'I've just come back to collect something.'

'Well, now you can go again.'

Nic leaned against the doorjamb, his arms folded across his chest, an annoying smile on his face. Well, she thought it was annoying, anyway. *He* was annoying.

'What's got you so riled?'

'None of your business,' she muttered, shoving a new prescription pad in her bag and searching crossly for her stethoscope before realising it was still around her neck. Wrenching it free, she tossed it inside before snapping her bag shut.

'Kirsty said I was to thank you.'

'Did she?'

'What am I to thank you for?'

'Why don't you ask her? The pair of you can do your own dirty work in future.'

Nic's eyes shone with laughter as she struggled to get her coat on. He crossed the room and took it from her. 'Let me help.'

'I can manage, thank you,' she said through gritted teeth, pulling it away from him and tossing it over her arm.

'*Sembrate bei guando siete arrabbiati, innamorata!*'

Hannah's temper flared anew. 'And stop talking to me in Italian when you know I don't bloody well understand what you are saying!'

'I said you look beautiful when you are angry, sweetheart,' Nic explained patiently, still smiling.

Face flushed, she stared up at him in confusion.

'Well, don't. Say it, I mean. In English or Italian. Now, please, get out of my way. I'm late.'

Gathering up her bag and notes, she stalked out of the room, fuming when she heard him chuckling behind her. In Reception, she slammed the tray of patient notes down on the counter, startling both Kirsty and Jane, who stared at her in amazement.

She glared at them. 'Something wrong?'

'No.' Kirsty grinned. 'Nothing at all.'

'Good. I'm going out.'

With as much dignity as she could muster, feeling stupid and not at all understanding her sudden burst of temper, Hannah hurried out to her car.

'Hannah was in earlier,' Jimmy McCall said in an increasingly rare wakeful spell, his breathing poor, his voice raspy and weak.

Nic smiled. 'She had a bit of a temper this morning.'

'Aye! Always had some fire about her. Used to, any road. Good to see.' Jimmy drew in a rasping breath and placed a gnarled, papery hand on Nic's. 'Hannah wasn't like this, not before she went away.'

'Don't try and talk now, Jimmy.'

'Must tell you. Important.'

Frowning, concerned how much Jimmy had deteriorated in the last week, Nic gently held his hand. 'OK.'

'I've known her since she was a wee one,' the dying man confided. 'So proud when she went to medical school.' He broke off to cough again, having a puff of oxygen before pushing the mask aside. 'When she came back she was different.'

'How was she different?' Nic prompted, curious but unwilling to tire Jimmy.

'She came home the first year or two, Christmas and such. Things seemed fine. She was leaning towards A and E then. Suddenly she changed. Said hospital life was not for her, she was training to be a GP and coming home.'

Nic helped him sip some water and waited as Jimmy caught his breath before he continued.

'When she first got back for good she was jumpy. Pale and thin. Sad most of all. Her father said it was like a light had been turned out inside her,' he went on, nodding his head slowly. 'It was true. These last years her life has been her work. Nothing else.'

While Jimmy paused to rest, Nic pondered on what Jimmy had said. It confirmed what he knew. Hannah had been hurt in some way. What he still didn't know was how. Did Jimmy know? But as keen as he was to learn more about Hannah's past, he was determined not to let the sick man tire himself.

'You sleep now, Jimmy.'

'No, no. Not long left,' he protested, and Nic leaned closer to hear as the man struggled to speak. 'Need to finish. Hannah like the daughter I never had. Her father was my best friend. I hate to see her so closed off. Part of her is in cold storage. Kindness itself with patients and staff, but not many could say they were close to her now. Something happened, Nic. I know it. But Hannah won't talk. She never speaks of her life away from here.'

'Why are you telling me this?'

'Hannah needs you.'

Nic was silent for a while, giving Jimmy time to rest, shaky fingers holding the oxygen mask to his face. 'What makes you think I could do anything, even if Hannah wanted me to?' he asked when the man rallied again.

'I may have only hours left, but I'm not blind. Or stupid.' Jimmy tried to smile. 'I see the way you look when you talk about her. And she's had some spark back since you came. She's lonely. I think you are, too, inside. You need each other. And now I've said too much. We never had this conversation, you understand?'

'I understand.'

Nic managed a smile, shaken by the older man's perception. Again it confirmed his own instincts about Hannah, but the missing pieces of the puzzle remained illusive. He spent some moments making Jimmy more comfortable, checking the oxygen and the settings on the morphine pump, those same instincts telling him the kindly man didn't have too much longer.

'You rest now, Jimmy,' he soothed. 'I'll come back later.'

'Not long. It's time. Don't let Hannah come,' he rasped.

'She'll want to see you.'

'No,' he protested in distress. 'Promise.'

Feeling bad, wondering if Jimmy would wake again, Nic squeezed his hand. 'I'll do all I can.'

Apparently satisfied, Jimmy relaxed. When he was confident Jimmy was sleeping peacefully, Nic slipped out of the room, smiling at the nurse now employed by the family to stay with the ill man all night.

'He's settled now. You'll call me as soon as there's any change?'

'I will, Doctor,' she promised, heading back into Jimmy's room to sit quietly with him.

* * *

When he got home that evening, he found Hannah sitting on the living room floor in front of the log fire, playing with Wallace. The little kitten was much more mobile now, quite a handful, keen to explore and usually getting himself into trouble. Despite his tiredness and his concern, Nic smiled. She looked up, her gaze wary, but all trace of her earlier temper gone from her eyes.

'Have you had supper?' she asked.

'No. I'll get something later.'

'There's some cauliflower cheese in the oven if you'd like it.'

Nic nodded, realising how long it was since he'd eaten and suspecting he had a long night ahead of him. 'Thanks, I think I will. Can I get you anything?'

'No, I'm fine.'

Hannah frowned as he left the room and she heard him go upstairs to change. He looked tired and worried about something. Was he thinking about his family? About Federica? The woman he'd loved, with whom he'd planned a family and a happy ever after, whose death had closed his heart? She swallowed the lump in her throat, dismissing a welter of confusing thoughts and unwanted emotions. Perhaps Nic was just wary after her strop that morning. It hadn't been fair, taking her temper out on him. She heard him moving about the kitchen a while later and was surprised when he carried his plate and a glass of water into the living room, sitting on the settee across from her to eat his meal. Hannah focused her concentration on Wallace, who pounced on the stands of wool she dangled for him. He still didn't look remotely lion-like, she mused, but Nic had been right—the little kitten was definitely a fighter.

'Thanks, Hannah, that was delicious.' Nic set his empty plate down, his smile tired.

'Can I get you some coffee?'

'Not right now.'

She watched as he sat back with a sigh, his long legs stretched out in front of him. He was very quiet tonight.

'Rough day?' she asked after a few moments of silence.

'I've had better.' He managed another smile. 'You?'

She flushed, thinking of her earlier behaviour. 'Likewise.'

'Who upset you this morning?'

'The blonde bombshell.'

'Who?'

'Sally Archibald.'

'I don't know her.'

Didn't he? Hannah looked at him with a frown. 'The barmaid at the village inn.'

'Oh.' Nic grimaced. 'I know who you mean.'

'I'm sure you've noticed her,' she muttered, with more sarcasm than she'd intended.

'Why do you say that?'

He didn't sound very pleased, she realised. 'Isn't that what most men go for? Petite, beautiful blondes?' she pressed, regretting the impulse when she saw his eyes narrow.

'I wouldn't know. I'm not most men. Don't stereotype me, Hannah, and file me away in some convenient box in your head.'

She swallowed, feeling well and truly put in her place. Out of the corner of her eye, she saw Nic get up and carry his plate and glass out to the kitchen. That hadn't been very clever of her, had it? Sitting cross-legged on the floor, she gathered Wallace onto her lap, stroking his soft, warm little body, surprised when Nic returned a couple of minutes later with two mugs of coffee.

'Thanks,' she murmured in confusion, setting hers on the table out of Wallace's reach.

Nic sat down in one of the armchairs closer to her. 'So what did she want?'

'Sally?' she queried nervously, and Nic nodded. 'You.'

'Excuse me?'

She almost smiled at the look of horrified surprise on his face. 'To quote Kirsty, Sally has "set her sights" on you.'

'*Il Dio lo aiuta.*' Seeing her frown, Nic smiled. 'God help me.'

'You might not need him. You've got Kirsty riding shotgun for you!'

Nic raised an eyebrow. 'Why?'

'You'll have to ask her. Sally showed up angling to see you so Kirsty shoved her on the end of my list.'

'I am sorry for that.'

Hannah shrugged, tickling Wallace under the chin, making him purr like a road drill. 'It doesn't matter.'

'I will sort things out with Kirsty and fight my own battles in future.'

'But—'

'Don't worry, *cara*, I'll deal with Sally if necessary.'

She wasn't sure whether to be relieved or not. The thought of Nic having anything to do with Sally still made her curiously disturbed and protective. Which was nonsense, of course. She took a sip of her coffee, nearly dropping the mug when she glanced at Nic and found him looking at her, interest in those watchful brown eyes. Oh, God, now what? she worried, setting her mug back down with shaky fingers.

'So,' he began, a slow, sexy smile pulling at the corners of his mouth.

Unnerved, Hannah shifted uncomfortably. 'So what?'

'What was it about Sally wanting me that had you so fired up?'

Damn the man! 'It wasn't that at all,' she denied airily, desperately trying to fabricate something plausible.

'Oh?'

'No. I'm afraid Sally's always rubbed me the wrong way. We just don't get on very well.'

'I see.'

He probably did, too, she realised, darting a hasty glance at him and seeing the glitter of amusement back in his eyes. She had another sip of coffee before returning her attention to Wallace. The little kitten seemed to have run out of steam at last and had curled up in her lap, fast asleep. Aware of Nic's gaze still on her, her own was drawn reluctantly back to him.

'I was just thinking,' he murmured, leaning back in the chair as she frowned at him.

'What about?'

'You. Why don't you have a man in your life?' Nic

regarded her for a moment, and she felt the familiar curl of heat inside her under the intensity of his gaze. 'You haven't answered my question.'

She looked down at Wallace again. 'Because I don't want one.'

'Why?'

'Why does there have to be a why?' she countered stiffly. 'I'm contented with my life as it is.'

'Are you?'

He always made her think about things she didn't want to face. With a sigh, she glanced at him. 'Why are you looking at me?'

'Because I like to.' He smiled, sitting forward, his elbows resting on his knees. 'You're a very beautiful woman.'

'Don't start that again,' she protested uncomfortably.

'In English or Italian?'

She scowled at him. 'Either.'

'I'm telling the truth.' He cupped her chin and she was forced to look at him. 'You are beautiful. And you're generous and kind, smart and caring, sexy and—'

'Oh, stop! That's ridiculous.'

'Someone has done a very thorough job on you, haven't they?'

His serious expression unsettled her and she moved

away, needing to escape his touch, passing Wallace to him as she stood up. 'I don't know what you mean.'

'Don't let them win, Hannah, and rob you of so much in life.'

She took the mugs out to the kitchen and washed up, her hands shaking, alarmed when Nic came through and settled Wallace down in his pen.

'I'm going to bed,' she announced, anxious to put some distance between them.

'*Desidero che potrei unirlo*,' he murmured, casting a mischievous glance at her as he told her how much he would like to join her.

Hands on hips she glared at him, infuriated again. 'What did you say?'

'I was talking to Wallace.'

'No, you weren't.' The gleam of wicked laughter in his eyes belied his innocent words. 'Nic—'

'I said, I wish you a good night.'

Hannah didn't believe him for a moment. As she climbed into bed a while later, she was sure she wouldn't sleep. Her mind seemed to be buzzing with so many disturbing and confusing things. All of which were Nic's fault. Frowning, she thumped the pillow and turned over. Did he flatter himself or what, thinking she'd been in a temper because Sally fancied him! Which, an annoying inner voice

taunted her, was precisely what had happened.
There was just no way she was going to admit she
wanted Nic herself. She didn't. And even if she did,
it was impossible.

Dawn was breaking when she woke up. She had
slept better than she'd expected, although she had
half stirred in the early hours, imagining she'd heard
the phone ring and the front door close.

Showered and dressed for morning surgery, she
went downstairs, chatting to Wallace as she put
some coffee on to percolate. She heard a car door
slam and then a key in the front door. So Nic had
gone out. She frowned. His bag hit the floor and
there was a rustle as he hung up his leather jacket.
She looked round with a smile as he came into the
kitchen but her smile faded when she saw him. He
looked terrible.

'Have you been out all night? I thought I heard the
phone but—' She broke off at the look on his face.
'What is it?'

He came towards her, eyes full of sadness and
concern. Fear curled through her as he slid his hands
up her arms to her shoulders.

'Nic?'

'I'm so very sorry, *innamorata*,' he murmured

hoarsely, the fingers of one hand stroking her face. 'Jimmy died a little while ago.'

She blinked back tears at the loss of the man she had known all her life and of whom she was so fond. 'I should have been there. Why didn't you call me?'

'Jimmy made me promise not to.'

'But why?' A wave of rejection swamped her. 'Why would he do that?'

'He cared for you. He didn't want you to see it at the end.'

'But it's my job… I wanted to be there for him.'

'I know, *cara*.'

Hannah was unable to prevent the tears escaping and she went, unresisting, into Nic's arms. He held her as she sobbed out her hurt and sadness, soothing her with words whose meaning she couldn't comprehend but which reached her in some elemental way, assuring her of his compassion, his own sadness.

As her first wave of tears subsided, he released her, handing her a tissue before he poured two mugs of coffee and encouraged her into the living room. Once there, he drew her down onto the settee.

'You knew, didn't you? Last night?' she accused, setting down her mug as her hands were too shaky to hold it.

'I suspected, yes.'

'I don't understand why he didn't want me there.'

He took her hand, his touch warm, both disturbing and comforting at the same time. 'Hannah, he loved you, he thought he was protecting you.'

'But I'm a doctor,' she protested.

'Yes, but you were also his friend.' Nic's thumb traced circles on her palm, distracting her. 'The daughter he never had.'

She stared at him in surprise. 'Jimmy said that?'

'He did.'

'But when? I...'

'I spent some time with him,' Nic confessed, surprising her anew. 'In the evenings, at weekends. At the beginning we'd play chess when he felt able, later we just talked, or I sat with him while he slept.'

The knowledge that Nic had done that for a man he scarcely knew touched her beyond measure. 'I didn't realise. But he shouldn't have been alone, with just a nurse,' she said, her voice unsteady.

'He wasn't alone, *cara*.'

'You were there?' She swallowed as he nodded. 'You did that for him?'

'And for you.'

Fresh tears pricked her eyes. 'For me?'

'I knew Jimmy was important to you. When I

found out that he had said you were not to be called, I thought you might feel easier if you knew I'd been there instead.'

Hannah didn't know what to say. It must have been hard for Nic to take on such a promise, to accept the responsibility of being with Jimmy, especially after all he himself had been through, losing those he loved. Tears spilled down her cheeks, not just for Jimmy and his death, but because Nic had done what he had done out of genuine kindness and care…had understood what this meant to her.

Now, as he held her, stroking her hair as she cried, she struggled to make sense of all the ramifications, not least the effect this man was having on her life.

CHAPTER SEVEN

'OUCH!' Nic complained as Wallace used his leg for climbing practice, sharp little claws digging through the denim of his jeans and into his thigh. 'Play fair, *uomo piccolo.*'

Gently he lifted Wallace off his leg, amazed how much the kitten had grown since the day he had found him so bedraggled and on the point of death. Stroking him, he set him on the bed, encouraging him to play with a little ball that had a bell inside it. Wallace swiped it with his paw and then pounced, rolling on his back with his prize. Laughing, Nic tickled his tummy.

Sobering, he glanced out of the window into the darkness. Not that he could have seen much had it been daytime as November was ending as wet and windy as it had begun, the ridge of the hills masked by low, grey cloud. The only sunshine had come, symbolically, on the day of Jimmy's funeral. With a frown Nic checked his watch. After six. He'd expected Hannah back by now. He hoped she was all right but she had been so sure she wanted to go alone to Jimmy's to meet his sister and collect some books that the kindly man had left to her.

Trying to concentrate, he turned his attention back to his research. He made some notes but all the time part of him was listening out for the sound of a car in the drive and the front door closing. When it finally came, half an hour later, a sigh of relief whispered from him.

'Hannah?' he called, hearing her footsteps on the stairs a few moments later.

'Hi,' she greeted him, hesitating just inside the door, a package tucked under her arm.

He scanned her face. 'You OK, *cara*?'

'I'm fine.' She moved across towards him, a wary look back in her eyes as she approached the bed, holding out the package. 'Here.'

'From you?' he questioned in surprise, setting his medical book aside.

'No, from Jimmy. Alice said he left instructions that you were to have it.'

Nic swallowed the lump in his throat and took the package, too overwhelmed to speak when he discovered the man he had known for far too short a time had left him his precious antique chess set. He glanced up at Hannah, knowing his feelings were reflected in his eyes, seeing her sad smile of understanding.

He cleared his throat. 'I don't know what to say.'

'You don't have to say anything,' she assured softly. 'We both know why Jimmy did it, what it meant to him.'

'And to me.'

'Yes.'

Nic watched as she crossed to the window and drew the curtains, his breath catching as his gaze ran over her. He almost wished she'd kept to the power suits. The sight of her legs and the curve of her rear in those jeans that moulded themselves like a second skin was driving him mad. And she'd left her hair loose for once. His fingers itched to feel it again.

Touched by how moved Nic was to receive Jimmy's final gift, Hannah fiddled with the curtains for a few moments, giving them both time to work through their emotions. When she turned from the window, heat curled through her at the look on Nic's face. There was a hunger in his eyes that scared her. Nervous, she looked beyond him to where Wallace was sleeping on his back, his little paws dangling in the air.

'You've worn Wally out, I see.'

'He's been using me as a climbing frame.' Nic smiled, mischief replacing the intensity in his gaze. 'I'm covered in scratches. Maybe you ought to look at them, make sure I don't get an infection, yes?'

Hannah didn't want to think about touching him again. 'No.'

'Shame,' he teased.

Shameless, Hannah corrected silently, trying not to smile. Nic had been amazing since Jimmy's death, never crowding her, yet always there if she needed anything. And he'd gone with her to the funeral. She knew it had been difficult for him, that he had been moved about Jimmy but also remembered his own tragic losses, too. Throughout it all, though, the tension remained between them, the air fizzing with electricity. Her awareness of him was becoming a major problem. She closed her eyes. What was she going to do about him?

'Did you collect your books?'

'Yes.' Nic's question dragged her mind away from her disturbing thoughts. 'There are more than I was expecting. I've left the boxes downstairs for now.'

'I'll help you with them later,' he offered softly, and she knew he understood what the things Jimmy had left meant to her.

'What are you working on?' she asked, as a charged silence threatened to stretch between them.

'I'm trying to get some information for a patient I saw today.' Frowning, he picked up his medical reference book. 'Do you know anything about gynaecomastia?'

'Male breasts? Not much. I saw a case once, while I was training. You?'

Nic shook his head. 'I know more now than I did this morning when the guy came in. I asked him to come back on Monday to give me forty-eight hours to do some research so I'll know how best to advise him. Here, look at this,' he invited, patting the bed beside him.

Interested, Hannah crossed the room, thinking how rumpled and attractive he looked, sitting there with one denim-clad leg tucked under him, the other dangling off the edge of the bed, his feet bare. Conscious of his nearness, the subtle aroma of sandalwood that had become so familiar, she forced herself to concentrate on the papers he handed her.

'I found an interesting site on the internet,' he told her now. 'If my patient has online access, this would be helpful for him.'

'What did you find when you examined him?'

'No evidence of tissue attached to muscle, no

lumps and no testicular tumours. But the breasts are noticeably very enlarged on both sides.'

Reading the advice from the sources he had already consulted, Hannah nodded. 'How old is he?'

'Twenty-one. The poor guy has been living with this for years, hoping it would end after puberty, too scared to ask for help,' he said, his sympathy evident in his voice.

'That's sad.' Hannah tucked some wayward strands of hair behind her ear, concentrating on the notes. 'Any reason he's come in now?'

Nic shrugged. 'It's affecting his whole life. He's too embarrassed to go out, to swim, to join in team sports, ask a girl out.'

'He's going to need a lot of emotional support, then, as well as any physical interventions.'

'I agree.'

She met Nic's gaze, warmed by the approval in his dark eyes. 'Any signs of the things it mentions here…liver disease or drug use, steroids or anything?'

'Not that I could tell on first consultation,' he replied, 'but I didn't know everything to look for this morning. My instinct says it is most likely to be hormonal.'

'So what are you going to do? Refer him to the endocrinologist?'

Nic nodded. 'If the patient will go. The question is, do we handle any counselling here, or do they deal with that at the hospital? And, if we do it, should it be before we refer him on?'

'You probably need to talk to him about that. If he's confident to go to the specialist now, that's great. If he needs more psychological support first, he can talk to Sarah,' Hannah said. 'How did he seem?'

'Scared but determined,' he assessed after some deliberation.

'It's an interesting one.'

Nic sighed, a pout of consideration on his lips. 'I might ring the endocrinologist on Monday and sound him out before I see the patient.'

'That's a good idea. Sorry I couldn't be more help.'

'You have helped.' She shivered as he took hold of her hand. 'It's good being able to discuss it. Thank you.'

'No problem,' she murmured, far too conscious of the distracting movement of his fingers on her skin.

Hannah groaned inwardly. Why did she always feel so ridiculously out of her depth with this man? If only she was more sophisticated and knew how do deal with him. Instead, Nic was two years younger than her in age but way ahead in terms of experience and being worldly wise. What she still could not understand was what he wanted with her, why he was interested.

'I was wondering,' she said, trying to inject some normality into her voice and, unsuccessfully, to extract her hand from his, 'if it was a time when you were not rostered on night calls, would you mind coping if I had a couple of days off?'

His fingers briefly stilled their caress but didn't release her. 'You want to go away?'

'Well, I just thought for a day or two,' she confirmed, disconcerted by the thread of disappointment in his voice.

'Of course, *cara*, we can manage, if you'd like a break.'

Against her better judgement, her gaze was drawn to his and a new prickle of awareness tingled down her spine as she looked into those dark, molten eyes. 'I, um, have a friend in Edinburgh and—'

'A friend?'

'Yes.' Why did she feel she had to explain everything? What business was it of his what she did and where she went? 'Lauren. Haven't I mentioned her?'

Nic's smile was more natural, almost relieved. 'No, I don't think you have.'

'We did some of our training together. She's in Paeds in Edinburgh now. I don't see her much but we email news occasionally and I go to Edinburgh once or twice a year.'

'And do you keep in touch with anyone else from your training days?' he queried lightly.

The question brought an uncomfortable lump to her throat. 'No.'

'Where was it you trained?'

'Birmingham,' she murmured, determined not to think about her time there. Or part of it, at least.

His fingers seemed to home in on the point at her wrist where her pulse had started beating erratically. 'A long way from home.'

'Mmm.' She cleared her throat. 'Anyway, I thought I'd go to Edinburgh next week, do some Christmas shopping, get my hair cut, see—'

'No! Don't you dare,' he interrupted, a horrified expression on his face.

Hannah hid a smile, some reckless streak making her tease him. 'I fancy a whole new look. Something short and chic and easier to manage.'

'You can tell your hairdresser that if he cuts off more than one centimetre he will have to answer to me,' he declared passionately, releasing her wrist but only so he could sink the fingers of both hands into her long, chestnut waves. 'Your hair is magnificent.'

Breathless, Hannah stared at him, shocked by

his intense reaction and by the feel of his hands on her. She hadn't meant things to go this far. 'Nic...' she whispered.

'Tell me you are joking.'

'I am,' she managed hoarsely. 'I'm only having it trimmed.'

'Promise me.'

Hannah nodded in response to his husky demand. When had he moved closer? Nervous, she looked at him, saw his eyes darken further with sultry desire as his gaze slid to her mouth and back to her eyes again. Oh, God, no! She didn't want him to kiss her again. Did she? Why had she been so foolish as to tease him? Heat curled through her at the determined intensity of his gaze. His hands in her hair tilted her head as he bent towards her, his mouth inexorably finding hers.

She whimpered, whether in protest or longing, she was too scared to question. Her lips parted under his, fire licking through her veins as he instantly took possession of her mouth, kissing her with melting intensity. Consumed. That was the only word for it, Hannah thought dazedly. It was as if he consumed her totally and completely. She was so out of practice, but no one had ever kissed her like this.

Nic groaned, one hand gliding down her body as

he lay back and drew her with him. She felt the solid breadth of his chest beneath her, felt him slide one leg between hers as his hand shaped the rounded swell of her rear before rising again, his fingers slipping under the hem of her top, caressing the hollow of her back. His touch on her bare skin made her gasp. She felt an unfamiliar ache low inside her and momentarily tried to assuage it by pressing herself more closely against him, feeling the evidence of his own arousal.

He broke the kiss, breathing heavily, pressing hot kisses to her throat as he whispered to her, his voice thick with desire. 'I want you so much.'

'No.' It was too much, too intense. Scared, she struggled against him, shocked by how quickly things had flared out of control. 'I can't! Stop it, please!'

'Hannah?' He relaxed his hold at once, eyes black with passion and confusion as he stared at her, hands cupping her face. 'Don't cry, *cara*.'

Panicked, Hannah pushed his hands away, scrambling to her feet, her legs feeling too shaky to hold her. Her lips were swollen and fiery from the intensity of his kiss. She stared at him, wiping away the tears she had not realised she was shedding, unaware how starkly her fear was etched on her face, how bruised her eyes were.

'I'm sorry,' she whispered, hearing him say something in Italian as she fled.

Nic swore succinctly in his native language as Hannah ran from him. What tortured her so much? One moment they were making progress, he was getting close to her and she was responding eagerly and then, in a heartbeat, some inner demon panicked her. Concerned, ignoring his own discomfort, he rose to his feet and walked along the landing to Hannah's room, unable to just let her rush away.

'Hannah?' he called, tapping on the door.

There was a long moment of silence before she replied. 'What?'

'I'm worried about you, *innamorata*.'

'I'm fine.'

'We both know that's not true.' He sighed, not knowing how to reach her. 'Can I come in?'

'No.'

'I'll just sit out here, then, and talk to you,' he said, lowering himself and leaning his back against the door.

There was another long pause before she spoke again. 'I'm sorry.'

'Stop apologising. Tell me what it is, *cara*.'

'I can't,' she refuted, her voice unsteady. 'It's not you, it's me.'

He rubbed a hand along his jaw. 'Hannah—'

'Please, Nic.'

'I want to understand. Let me help you.'

Her reply was slow in coming and not what he wanted to hear. 'I'm sorry. Leave me alone now.'

'If that's what you want.' Frustrated, hurting for her, he stood up, a frown on his face. 'Call me if you need anything.'

He didn't see her the next day. He'd planned to go hill walking with a few of his new friends from the village and, while tempted to cancel, he decided to give Hannah the space she had asked for. Whatever spooked her was something deep rooted and he wasn't going to uncover it in five minutes. Or by pushing her too hard. At first he had imagined there had been some love affair gone wrong, but doubts were creeping in. Her reactions appeared too extreme for that. When he arrived back at the house after dark, there was no sign of her and no light coming from her room. But when she had left the house before him on Monday morning, his suspicions that she was avoiding him increased.

At his desk, he put a call through to the endocrinologist, pleased to secure the information and advice he needed for when he saw his troubled patient later in the morning.

Frowning, he turned to his computer. '*Are you all right?*' he emailed, waiting impatiently for Hannah to reply, knowing she was mere feet away from him. Finally a ping announced the arrival of a message in his inbox.

'*Yes. How did you go with the endocrinologist?*'

OK, so she wanted to ignore what was happening. At least she was talking to him. Sort of. Following her lead, he gave her a brief rundown on what the specialist had told him. '*I'll discuss the options with the patient later on,*' he finished.

'*That's good, I hope all goes well. If it's OK, I think I'll go to Edinburgh today. The rota is covered for the next couple of nights so you don't need to worry,*' she informed him.

'*I'll worry about you,*' he emailed back, frustrated that she was running away. Again.

'*Don't.*'

He couldn't help it. Despite being so busy covering all the surgeries, clinics and home visits, the days passed with painful slowness while she was away, the house feeling empty, even with Wallace's increasingly active companionship.

Scared to look too closely at his own emotions and how involved he was becoming, Nic counted the minutes until she came home.

It was dark when Hannah drove back to Lochanrig on Wednesday, her car full of parcels. She let herself in, thankful Nic was not yet back from the surgery. The time away had done nothing to resolve things in her head, she admitted, making several trips to carry everything inside. While shopping, along Princes Street and many other nooks and crannies she knew in the city, visiting the hairdresser, and meeting up with Lauren, when they had gone for a meal at a renowned Indian restaurant on Dalry Road, and caught up on their news, thoughts of Nic had nagged constantly, and Jimmy's words had plagued her, too.

She was greeting Wallace when she heard Nic return. Her eyes closed for a moment as she steeled herself to face him again after the disastrous events of the weekend. He had every right to be angry with her. That he remained so understanding and con-cerned almost made her feel worse.

'Hi.'

The sound of his husky, accented voice sent a

prickle of heat along her spine and she turned, not quite able to meet his gaze. 'Hi.'

'How was Edinburgh?'

'Too busy and crowded. But I did the things I wanted to do.'

'You kept your promise with your hair.'

Her gaze clashed with his and she saw the relief mixed with the amusement in his dark eyes. 'I was never going to cut it,' she murmured, a flush warming her cheeks.

'*Dio grazie.*' A smile curved that sensual mouth. 'And did you see your friend?'

Hannah struggled to drag her gaze and her thoughts away from his mouth and how it had felt on hers. 'Lauren? Yes, we had a meal last night,' she managed, her voice rough.

'Hannah—'

'I've put something on for supper,' she broke in, scared he was going to bring up anything personal again. 'How did things go with your gynaecomastia patient?'

She heard Nic sigh and he moved to pick up Wallace to make a fuss of him. 'I am going to refer him to the endocrinologist. While he's waiting for an appointment, he's going to talk with Sarah and come and see me again.'

'I'm glad.'

'I'll go and get changed,' Nic decided, handing Wallace over to her, his dark eyes serious. 'It's good to have you back, we missed you.'

It was good to be back, Hannah allowed, though she was far less willing to admit the fact that she had missed him, too. As the days passed, she felt calmer and although she knew it was a temporary respite and he would not give up, Nic respected her need for space and didn't press her for any answers to his questions.

'Doesn't it look festive?' Kirsty demanded, casting a satisfied eye over the Christmas decorations around the reception and waiting areas.

'You've all done a good job.' Hannah smiled, hiding her personal feelings about Christmas— lonely and sad since the loss of her parents.

'Nearly time for our meal out!' Jane grinned as she joined the rest gathered in the staffroom.

'You are coming, aren't you, Nic?' Shona asked.

Hannah saw him glance up from his coffee. 'If I'm invited,' he agreed, his smile making her stomach churn.

'Oh, Hannah, haven't you mentioned it?' Kirsty chastised. 'Of course you're invited, Nic! It's the one time of the year we all go out and have a meal and a drink together!'

'I'll look forward to it.'

'There's New Year as well,' Morag reminded them. 'Is everyone going to the dance?'

There was a chorus of agreement and Debbie looked at Hannah. 'You'll come, won't you?'

'No,' she refused, 'not this time.'

Morag frowned. 'You say that every year.'

'Please, come,' Jane begged.

'No, I'm afraid not.'

'You've got a special invite!' Kirsty chipped in, a mischievous glint in her eyes. 'Sandy Douglas wants you to go with him. I said I'd tell you.'

Hannah stared at her in horrified surprise. 'Well, you can thank him but the answer is no.'

'He's been sweet on you for years,' Kirsty teased, and the others laughed.

'Don't be silly, Kirsty,' Hannah responded, feeling distinctly uncomfortable. Out of the corner of her eye she saw Nic rise to his feet and wash his mug, a frown on his face. 'I'm not interested in Sandy Douglas and I never will be.'

An awkward silence followed her statement and Hannah knew they were all looking at her, all wondering, imagining. She swallowed, wishing she could make a dignified exit.

'Hannah, have you got a moment to spare before surgery? I need to ask your advice about a patient,' Nic asked, heading for the door.

A wave of relief swamped her and she all but shot out of her chair. 'Yes, of course.'

She followed him into his consulting room and he turned to face her, leaning against his desk. The scrutiny of his dark gaze made her fidget.

'You, um, wanted to ask me something?'

'No.' He smiled.

'But you said…'

He shrugged. 'I thought you wanted rescuing.'

'Oh.' Colour washed her cheeks. 'Thank you.'

'Who is this Sandy Douglas?'

Her colour deepened. 'Don't, Nic, please. He's just a guy I was at school with. We went out a couple of times when we were about sixteen, that's all. A lifetime ago. It's nothing,' she insisted, not sure why she wanted him to understand.

'So when is this meal out for all of us?'

'December the twenty-third. And I didn't deliberately not invite you—I'd forgotten all about it,' she explained, relieved he'd changed the subject.

His smile crinkled the corners of his eyes. 'Don't worry, Hannah.'

'I meant to say,' she rushed on, 'if you want some

time off to go back to Italy for Christmas or anything, just ask.'

'I don't. But thank you. I already have plans for Christmas.'

'Oh, of course.' Hannah fought down a sinking feeling of disappointment. 'That's fine.'

'I'm really looking forward to it.'

Did he have to rub it in? 'That's good.'

Straightening, he stepped closer, making her nervous, then his fingers trailed down her cheek, leaving her skin burning from his touch. 'I'm planning on spending my Christmas with you and Wallace.' He smiled, moving round his desk to sit down.

Hannah returned to her own consulting room feeling ridiculously pleased. If she could just stop things getting too personal between them, maybe this Christmas would be much less lonely than usual. A curl of anticipation inside her, she forced herself to concentrate on another busy surgery.

'I've had a letter from your optician, telling me that he found some abnormalities when you had your recent eye test, Mr Scott,' Hannah explained gently, regarding the elderly man who sat across from her, his wife next to him, both anxious.

Mr Scott nodded, his voice gruff. 'Yes, he said something about the pressure?'

'That's right. It's a classic sign of chronic simple glaucoma. Increased pressure in the fluids in the eye damages the optic nerve. You may have noticed that your field of vision has been narrowing.'

'Will it get better, Doctor?' Mrs Scott asked, her hand nervously reaching for her husband's.

'I'm afraid the damage already caused is irreversible,' she told them as gently as she could. 'But we can do things to minimise and slow down any further deterioration.'

The elderly couple glanced at each other and Hannah felt sorry for them. It was always worrying when something went wrong, especially with the eyesight. She didn't want to alarm them at this stage with the knowledge that his condition could ultimately lead to blindness later in his life. She hoped it wouldn't happen.

'What I'll do,' she continued, 'is refer you to the eye clinic, Mr Scott. They will do some more detailed tests and look in your eyes to assess any damage and monitor the pressures. The specialist will likely prescribe you some drops to put in your eyes each day from now on and he'll write to me and let me know his findings. Is there anything else you want to ask me?'

'You say I'll have to have drops?' the elderly man asked worriedly.

'The condition can usually be controlled with eye drops, although you will probably have some deterioration over the years. You'll be monitored by us and the eye clinic. And if you have any children or grandchildren, do let them know about your condition. It can be congenital so it is important for close relatives to have regular eye tests.'

The couple rose to their feet, managing smiles. 'Thank you, Dr Frost, you've been very kind.'

'It's no problem,' she assured them, showing them out. 'Always get in touch if you are worried.'

Surgery over, Hannah went out to do a few house calls and she was running late when she headed back to Lochanrig.

'What on earth…?' she exclaimed, as she approached the village.

The scene was chaotic. Vehicles had been abandoned in the road and up ahead a lorry, one of the loaders that carried trees away from the forestry felling operations, was at an angle across the road, its nose buried in the front of the newsagent's, the squashed remains of a car poking out from beneath it.

'Oh, my God.'

Hannah grabbed her medical bag, and ran to the scene, pushing her way determinedly through the people who milled about, telling them to move further back, away from the dangerous lorry, which rested precariously, making horrible creaking, groaning noises and threatening to shift at any moment.

'What happened here?' she demanded, seeing Jane, the surgery's young receptionist, standing nearby.

'I was g-going to the post office. The lorry was coming through and it just s-swerved out of control, hit a car, went over the pavement and p-ploughed into the shop,' she explained, visibly shaken. 'We've c-called an ambulance and everything.'

'How many hurt?'

'A few cuts and bruises. We th-think the lorry driver m-must have died at the w-wheel.'

Hannah gave Jane a quick once-over. Clearly the girl was very shocked. 'Go back to the surgery and sit down for a while with a cup of tea,' she instructed, looking around and seeing that Morag, their practice nurse, was on scene and trying to calm a hysterical young woman. 'And, Jane, ask Nic to come down with some more supplies.'

'B-but he's already here.'

The girl stared at her with frightened eyes. Something about her expression caused a knot of fear to curl through Hannah's stomach and a chill creep up her spine.

'What do you mean, Jane?'

'N-Nic,' the girl confirmed, her voice trembling. 'He's u-under the lorry.'

CHAPTER EIGHT

'*MALEDIZIONE*!'

Swearing under his breath, Nic wriggled through the tangled mess under the lorry in an attempt to reach the child in the pushchair who had been swept underneath in the carnage and was stuck fast. He stopped, holding his breath, his heart racing, as the lorry shifted above him, twisting the remains of the empty car that was now mangled beyond recognition.

Dragging his kit with him, he inched his way further in, able in the light of his torch beam to see the battered pushchair and a pair of pink-clad feet sticking out. It seemed to take for ever to crawl the rest of the way and get some kind of view of the little girl, but when he did, he could see the serious-ness of the situation at once. As well as a head wound, which was bleeding profusely but seemed superficial, she appeared to have a nasty leg break and other cuts and bruises. By far the worst, he feared, was the penetrating trauma to her chest.

'*Maledizione!*' he repeated, hearing the audible sucking of air as he reached her.

It was clear the parietal pleura was broken and open, allowing the pleural cavity exposure to the outside air. He had to treat that quickly, before the lung fully collapsed. Tucking the torch awkwardly under his chin, he opened his bag and searched for a sterile occlusive dressing and some tape.

'Nic?'

Dio! What was Hannah doing here? 'Don't you dare come near this lorry,' he shouted to her.

'What have you got?'

'Open pneumothorax.'

He didn't waste time on further explanations. With no sign of any foreign bodies apparent on his examination, he worked swiftly to cover the wound, taping it down on three sides, creating a valve flap of the fourth side that prevented air getting in but allowed any excess air out. Satisfied the temporary action had improved things for the time being, he shifted uncomfortably in the cramped space to assess the girl's other injuries, concerned that she was conscious and watching him, but apparently traumatised. She seemed to be able to move but was mute with fear.

'OK, *ragazza piccola*. We'll soon have you out, little girl.'

He managed to get a line in and, after giving some analgesia, he set up some fluids for the shock and blood loss. Turning his attention to her head, he confirmed his first assessment that the scalp wound was superficial and no other serious injuries seemed to have occurred to her head or face. Straining in the confines available to him, he shone his torch in her eyes, relieved to find the pupils even and reacting normally.

Huge, tear-filled blue eyes focused on him and he smiled, gently stroking her cheek with one finger. 'My name is Nic. You're doing well, *ragazza piccola.*'

Having dressed the head wound, he shifted down to take a closer look at her lower leg. It was clearly broken below the knee, but he was thankful there was no bone showing.

'Hannah?'

'I'm here,' she responded, far too quickly.

'I told you to move away.'

'I wouldn't have heard you, then, would I?'

He let the snappy riposte go for now. 'Any sign of the fire service or the paramedics?'

There was a brief pause. 'Ambulance just pulling up and fire service ETA two minutes. What do you need?'

'A lower leg gutter or vacuum splint for a small

child,' he requested. 'But don't you bring it. This lorry could shift again at any time.'

He frowned when she didn't answer, but as if he had brought about his own fears, creaking and groaning marked more movement in the wreckage. As he shuffled to try and protect the child from further harm, he tore his arm on some jagged metal from the mangled car. Swearing at the lancing pain, he had to force himself free, feeling blood flow down his arm.

'Nic, are you OK?'

'I'm fine,' he lied, gritting his teeth as he moved, hearing the anxiety in Hannah's voice.

'We're pushing the splint in now,' she called. 'Can you see it?'

'Yes.'

As he reached for the pack, ignoring the pain in his arm, there was a thud as he smacked his face on a piece of wreckage.

'*Merda!*'

'What happened?'

'Nothing to worry about.'

His fingers tested his cheekbone but he couldn't find anything broken. Muttering darkly in Italian, he grabbed the gutter splint and crawled back to the child, taking the vinyl-covered pad and wrapping it round the damaged leg as gently as he could, fastening the Velcro straps in place.

'The fire service is here. They're going to use air bags to make the lorry safe,' Hannah called. 'Can you come out now?'

'No.'

'Nic…I can smell petrol.'

Now she mentioned it, so could he. He could also hear how scared she was. 'We'll be all right, *cara*. You move away now, please.'

It seemed to take for ever waiting for the air bags to be inflated and the scene made safe. *Dio*. He wished Hannah hadn't told him about the petrol, he'd been anxious enough as it was. Talking softly to the little girl, he checked her injuries constantly, paying extra attention to her breathing and the temporary repair he'd made to the sucking chest wound. There was more that needed doing, but the cramped conditions made it impossible.

'Hi, Doc,' a firefighter greeted him, wriggling in beside him. 'I'm Drew. You OK?'

'I've been better.'

'What have we got?'

Nic ran swiftly through the child's injures. 'She's conscious but quiet. I can't get her out of the pushchair, the way it's pinned. It's going to need cutting out.'

'We can do that.'

'And the petrol?' Nic said.

Drew grinned. 'All in a day's work!'

'Right.' Nic smiled back. 'How long?'

'Hard to say. You want to come out now?'

Nic shook his head, looking at his small patient. 'No, I'm here to the end.'

'OK, Doc.' Drew gave him a pat on the shoulder. 'Back soon.'

It took nearly half an hour of skilful work before the child was free and able to be slid out to the waiting paramedics. By the time Nic scrambled out, she was already on a stretcher and being loaded into the ambulance, her shocked and sobbing mother being helped inside by Morag. He gave the paramedics a quick debrief on what he had done.

'You coming with us?' one of them asked, gesturing to his arm. 'That could use some attention.'

'No, I'll be OK here. Thanks.'

He watched the ambulance drive away, hoping the child would recover well. Turning, his gaze clashed with a furious green one. Hannah looked fit to burst, he realised, watching as she stalked across to him, her face deathly pale.

'What the hell did you think you were doing?' she demanded angrily.

'The same thing you would have done had you been here first.'

He saw confusion mix with the anger and fright. 'That's not the point. You could have been killed.'

'It's nice to know you care about me,' he teased, trying to lighten the situation.

'This isn't funny.'

'Hannah, I'm fine.'

'Like hell.' Her stormy gaze raked over him, a suspicion of tears glinting in her eyes. 'Go back to the house and get out of those things. You're bleeding. I'll get some stuff and take a look at you.'

He wanted to argue but his arm throbbed like hell and his clothes were wet with a combination of blood, rain and fuel. What she said made sense. After a moment's further hesitation, he collected his things and accepted a lift home from the local policeman.

'Nic?' Hannah called as she let herself into the house a short while later.

She was still shaking. She would never forget the moment when Jane had told her Nic was under the lorry. For one terrifying instant she had thought he'd been involved in the accident, that she was going to lose him, the shock bringing home how much he had come to mean to her in the last weeks.

When it had become clear he had wriggled under there to get to the trapped child, she had been angry, scared, relieved and desperately confused about her own emotions. Sighing, she walked up the stairs and, hearing running water, went along the landing to his room.

'Nic?' She tapped on the open door. 'Are you OK?'

The noise of the water stopped. 'I will be just a minute.'

'Come down to the kitchen when you're ready.'

The short wait stretched like hours. She double-checked her medical bag making sure she had everything she could possibly need. When she heard his footsteps on the stairs, she sucked in a breath and braced herself, only to find she was completely unprepared for the sight of him. He'd had the sense to put a pack and waterproof dressing on his arm before he'd had a shower, she noted absently. Other than that, he had pulled on a pair of disreputable jeans…and nothing else. His feet were bare, and so was the rest of him.

'Sit down,' she instructed, her voice sounding alien to her own ears.

She turned away and closed her eyes, but even so the image of his perfectly sculpted chest and arms seemed imprinted on her brain—olive-toned skin drawn over muscle, a light dusting of dark hair tapering from his chest down his abdomen to the un- fastened waistband of his jeans, broad shoulders, his dark hair still damp from the shower.

Forcing herself to turn round, she evaded his gaze as she stepped closer to examine the damage. He had some superficial cuts and grazes on his face, forearms and hands, and a nasty bruise was swelling up along one cheekbone. It was disconcerting, leaning in close to him, checking for signs of grit, glass or metal fragments in the cuts. She was too close. She could feel the warmth of him, feel the draught of his breath, scent his aroma…clean male skin and sandalwood. Then there was that mouth, temptingly close. Disconcerted, her gaze strayed to his as she stepped back, finding him watching her through dark, sultry eyes.

'The abrasions don't look too bad,' she informed him stiffly. 'I'll clean them up when I've had a look at that arm.'

Which meant she had to touch him. Briefly she closed her eyes again. She couldn't do this. For goodness' sake, she was a doctor, she berated herself. What was wrong with her? She did this sort of thing all the time, saw all kinds of people in all states of undress. Just think of Nic as any other patient, the same as when he was ill, her rational brain instructed, but the wires seemed to get crossed somewhere along the line, and she couldn't visualise him like that at all. Not now. Hannah swallowed. She was a professional, it was time she acted like one.

Pulling herself together, she gently removed the temporary dressing, her fingers gliding over the warm skin and smooth muscle of his upper arm as she examined the nasty-looking cut. She heard Nic's hiss of breath and glanced at him.

'I'm sorry, did I hurt you?'

Smouldering dark eyes looked back at her. 'No.'

'There are no fragments,' she told him briskly, withdrawing her fingers as if his flesh burned them. 'But it will need a clean before I stitch it.'

'Fine.'

She turned back to her bag and pulled on a pair of latex gloves. In case of cross-infection, she told herself, knowing it was a lie. She just didn't think she could touch that bare flesh again and stay sane. 'I'll give you a local,' she told him, her voice sounding strange.

'It's OK.'

Frowning, she turned to face him. 'Nic, that's silly—'

'Just do it,' he insisted, his voice rough.

Her gaze met his and she couldn't recognise the disturbing expression in his eyes. 'Nic?'

'Hannah. Do it.'

'Is this some stupid macho thing?' she grumbled, readying the items she needed, unable to understand him. 'What's the point of this? Haven't you been enough of a hero for one day?'

She took a deep breath. Everything was ready, but anxiety and confusion made her edgy. With infinite care she cleaned the wound, feeling him tense, knowing it must hurt. She prepared to stitch, her fingers not as steady as she would wish. And the gloves made not a scrap of difference to her awareness, either. Hesitating, she looked at him, desperate not to hurt him, but he gave no ground at all, his expression implacable.

Hannah sucked in a breath. Stupid, idiot man. She hooked a chair closer with her foot and sat down. Working as carefully and gently as she could, she began to close the jagged wound with a row of neat stitches, aware every time he winced, tears stinging her eyes as she glimpsed his rigid jaw and bruised, battered face. Her gaze strayed to his chest, the rhythmic, slightly rapid rise and fall as he breathed. Hannah swallowed. Stop looking at his body and concentrate on what you are doing, she berated herself, thankful her task was nearly over. The stitches finished, she covered the wound with a sterile dressing and held it in place with a bandage. Pushing back her chair, she cleaned the cuts and abrasions on his face, before peeling off her gloves and tossing them aside.

'All done. You should have some antibiotics, though. Is your tetanus up to date?'

'Yes' His unfathomable gaze met hers, increasing her awkwardness and discomfort. 'Thank you.'

'OK.'

She looked down into his dark eyes, still unsure what fired his intense expression. Turning her back on him to tidy up, she discovered her hands were shaking.

'Hannah—'

'I have to get back for afternoon surgery now,' she forestalled him, keeping herself busy and avoiding looking at him again.

'I can come in and do my list,' he argued.

Annoyed, she turned to face him, finding he was back on his feet and closing in on her. 'Don't be silly.'

'*Cara*, I'm fine, really. It's nothing some pain-killers and a few days' healing will not fix. I'm not an invalid.'

'No, you just could have been dead. It was a recklessly stupid thing to do.'

'And you would have done the same, no?' He took her shaking hands in his. 'I'm sorry you were frightened.'

'Don't flatter yourself.'

She blinked back a fresh sting of tears as his gaze held hers and his voice dropped. 'You do this all the time, hide your feelings. I can see when you're scared, when you are hurting and putting on a brave front and need someone but won't admit it.'

'I don't,' she refuted, her throat tightening under his speculation, realising this was no longer just about today's events. 'Nic…'

'You think I don't worry or get scared for you when you are out on an emergency call, crawling around some gully or a car wreck on the motorway? Why do you find it so hard to admit you have feelings, or that other people have feelings for you?'

'Don't.'

'When are you going to trust me, *innamorata*?'

She fought to resist his persuasive appeal, trying without success to free her hands from his. 'I've told you, it's not you, it's me.'

'I can't help put things right until I know what went wrong.'

'There's nothing to put right,' she insisted, unable to meet his dark and compelling gaze.

'Believe me, Hannah, there is. And before I leave here, I'm going to prove it to you.'

Nic's words stayed with her in the busy days ahead. While the local community treated him as a hero, much to his embarrassment, she still trembled when she thought of the risk he had taken, equally disturbed at how emotionally involved she was becoming.

'Come on, sleepyhead.'

A husky voice permeated her consciousness. 'Hmm?'

'Time to wake up,' the voice cajoled. 'Hurry, *cara*, or I'll be tempted to climb in there with you!'

'What?' Hannah's eyes flew open, her gaze focusing on Nic's laughing dark eyes as he leaned over her bed. She grabbed the duvet, holding it under her chin. 'What are you doing?'

'It's after ten and we have chores to do.'

'We do?'

He set a wriggling Wallace down on top of her. 'I'll leave our little friend to hassle you awake, but I'll be back if you're not downstairs in half an hour.'

Still muzzy from sleep, Hannah was too slow to react as he closed the last of the distance and dropped a lingering, toe-curling kiss on her startled lips before leaving the room. God, what was going on? She yawned, trying to remember what day it was. Christmas Eve. And they'd been to the staff dinner the night before. Oh, hell and damnation. She had the most terrible recollection that she might have kissed him!

Forcing her mind to function, she went back over her memories of the evening. They'd had a good meal, shared plenty of laughter. She'd stuck to mineral water and Nic had only had a couple of glasses of red wine, but some of the others had been a bit merry, teasing Jane about her upcoming wedding in February. She remembered going to the bar to buy a round of drinks and being hassled by some creep, then Nic had materialised from nowhere and rescued her. When they'd got home, he'd said she could give him a goodnight kiss in payment.

'I won't touch!' he'd teased, slipping his hands in his trouser pockets.

Clearly he'd issued the challenge, never expecting her to act on it. So why the hell had she? She remembered standing on the stairs, a couple of risers above him, turning, stepping down one and pressing her lips to his. He was shocked, if his indrawn breath had been any guide. There had been no point of contact apart from their lips. Nothing to detain her. Nothing to prevent her from pulling back, as she had intended to when she had embarked on her foolish deed. But the peck she had planned had been forgotten the moment his mouth had opened under hers, hot and demanding and, oh, so seductive. Nothing had detained her but his magnetism and her weakness. Dear God, whatever had possessed her?

'Wally, don't sit on my head,' she groaned, gently lifting him off and struggling to sit up. 'I can't see.'

Setting the playful kitten on the bed, she pushed the tangled fall of hair out of her face and looked at the clock. Nic was right. It was after ten. But what chores did they have to do? She frowned, unable to remember anything outstanding from work. Still, she didn't put it past him to come back if she didn't get up, and that thought alone was enough to have her scrambling from the bed. She went to have a quick shower and then returned to dress, selecting jeans, boots and a warm, russet-coloured, hooded sweater that came halfway down her thighs. Dragging a brush through her wayward chestnut waves, she drew her hair back in a ponytail. A quick sweep of a honey stick lip balm across her lips and a squirt of perfume and she was ready.

Wallace scrambled backwards down the sheer

cliff face that was the side of the bed and padded after her on stubby little legs, determined not to be left behind as she headed for the stairs. 'Not down here, little man,' she told him, scooping him up, frightened he would fall.

Nic was in the kitchen and he looked up with a smile, the bruise on his cheek slowly fading. 'Five minutes to spare, *cara*,' he teased, checking his watch.

'I need breakfast,' Hannah warned, setting Wallace on the floor.

'Coming up. Toast, honey, coffee and juice, yes?'

The warmth in his gaze made her tingle. 'Thank you.'

'Pleasure.'

'So,' she asked, trying to steer things away from dangerous territory, terrified he would refer to what had happened last night, 'what are these chores we apparently have to do?'

'Wait and see.'

Hannah frowned at Nic's mysterious smile. 'I was looking forward to my day off.'

'It's not work,' he promised.

'Is this a bike thing?'

Nic sat on a chair opposite, his presence unnerving her. 'Not today, don't worry.'

'Oh.' Hannah spread honey on her toast, secretly

regretting that he'd never asked her for another outing after that one time. 'That's OK.'

'You're disappointed, aren't you?'

Her gaze skittered away from the knowing look on his face. 'Not at all.'

'We can share a ride together any time you want, *innamorata*,' he murmured huskily. 'You only have to ask.'

The breath locked in her lungs. Now she was very much afraid they were not talking about motorbikes at all. Deciding it would be much safer if she stopped verbally sparring with him, Hannah ducked her head and concentrated on finishing her breakfast.

'So where are we going?' she asked a while later, as they headed off in Nic's car.

'You'll soon find out.'

Before long he turned down a muddy track leading to a forestry plantation. 'Christmas trees?' she asked in surprise.

'Exactly!'

'I don't usually bother.'

'This year we are having a proper tree,' he decreed. 'With roots. So it can be planted afterwards in the garden.'

So she'd always have to look at it and remember

the Christmas Nic was there? A lump lodged in her throat. 'But—'

'Enough. It's Wallace's first Christmas. We can't let him down.'

Laughter bubbled inside her. 'That is so ridiculous!'

She was still giggling as Nic, trying to look affronted, drew the car to a halt next to others near a wooden hut that served as a sales office. 'You are going to be in so much trouble, *cara*,' he warned, dark eyes glinting with laughter.

Very much afraid she already was, she made no further comment and trailed in his wake as he set off to examine the rows of trees. It took an inordinate amount of time to choose one.

'They all look the same,' she complained after a while, earning herself another warning look. She would have just picked the first thing and been on her way, but Nic examined one after the other and she shook her head in bemusement.

'This one.' He finally selected a freshly dug specimen, a good seven feet high with a healthy root system. 'Perfect!'

'You shouldn't be carrying it with your bad arm.'

Nic shook his head dismissively. 'My arm is nearly healed. You'll be taking the stitches out in a day or two, no?'

'No. Morag's offered to do that.'

'Coward,' he teased, a knowing smile curving his mouth.

'Anyway, that tree is much too big.'

Nic's smile widened at her unsubtle change of subject. 'Nonsense. It has a beautiful shape—like you, *innamorata*!' he added in a husky aside as he walked past her and headed for the sales office.

Disconcerted, she followed him. Slowly but surely he was wearing down her resistance and she would have to redouble her guard if she didn't want to get into further trouble. And what if she did want to? She tried to push traitorous thoughts aside as she helped Nic tie their deliciously scented tree to the roof rack before they headed back to Lochanrig. She could never deny what an excellent doctor he was, but on a personal level he disturbed and unsettled her more every day. She was scared of the things he made her think and feel. Her life might not have been exciting before he'd arrived but she had felt safe. Now Nic not only challenged her present, he was stirring up painful things from the past she did not want to face.

'If you want to fetch a tub from the garage to put the tree in, I'll go and find the decorations,' she suggested when they arrived home.

'No problem.'

Wallace was excited by the strange activity and had to be removed from the various boxes of baubles and tinsel on numerous occasions.

'You're a menace, Wally.' Hannah laughed, rescuing him for the umpteenth time and sitting back on her heels on the floor to cuddle him.

Draping a strand of lights through the tree, Nic smiled. 'He has to have his first vaccination next week.'

'I can't bear to think of him having his injections. He's so tiny.'

'I know.' Nic grinned at her. 'I feel like an anxious papa!'

'When does he have the second vaccination?'

'Three weeks after the first one, when he's twelve weeks.'

Sighing, she set Wallace down to play with a toy and handed Nic the star for the top of the tree. She watched as he climbed the steps and reached to fix it in place, swallowing at the way his jeans tightened across his muscled thighs and taut rear, his jumper riding up to reveal a brief but tantalising glimpse of olive-toned flesh. What was happening to her? She turned away, seeking to banish the thoughts and deny the simmering awareness she had no wish to feel.

* * *

Nic woke on Christmas morning sensing that something was different. Frowning, he crossed to the window and looked out on a magical snowy landscape. Everything sounded hushed and muted, while a pale sun cast a clear and shimmering light, prisms glinting off suspended flakes and icicles that hung from the bare twigs of trees and the edges of gutters and garden railings.

Hearing noises downstairs, he dressed hurriedly and went down to find Hannah busy in the kitchen. She was wearing jeans and a fleecy top and she looked good enough to eat. His hands itched to hold her, but he was still wary of overstepping her boundaries, even though temptation often got the better of him.

'Good morning.'

She turned at the sound of his voice and gave a wary smile. 'Hi.'

'It snowed!'

'It looks lovely, doesn't it?' she agreed, glancing out of the window. 'Not so good if we get a callout, though.'

'Don't even think it,' he groaned.

'Someone, somewhere is bound to fall off their new bike or get their finger stuck in some new toy,' she teased. 'It happens every Christmas.'

Nic shook his head. 'Not today.'

'We'll see!'

'You're not planning to be working in here all day, are you?' He frowned, helping himself to some coffee.

'The turkey won't cook itself.'

'Then I help, yes? And we get the chores done sooner. Tell me what I can do.'

Hannah shook her head. 'Why don't you go and occupy Wallace before he wrecks all the presents under the tree?'

'Then we can open them, yes?'

'Go away!' She laughed, reaching out to give him a push. Nic caught her hand, drawing her towards him, seeing uncertainty shadow her eyes. 'Nic?'

'Happy Christmas, *cara*.'

As her lips parted to respond to his greeting, he bent his head, unable to resist another moment. His mouth caressed hers, his tongue beginning a leisurely exploration, finding her as sweet as he remembered. As ever when he touched her, it threatened to flare out of control in an instant, and he was fighting his own need. He couldn't rely on the pain of stitches without local anaesthetic every day to stop himself giving in to temptation and reaching for her. Now there was nothing he wanted more than to back her up against the table and have her wrap her legs around him as he united them, but it wasn't going to happen, not until her ghosts had been laid to rest. He could feel it in her now, the initial spontaneous response followed by the awakening of whatever haunted her. She was pulling back, emotionally and physically. Reluctantly, his breathing as ragged as hers, he let her go, looking down at her flushed face and the confusion in her gold-flecked green eyes.

'I'm going,' he promised, his voice rough with unfulfilled need.

It would be a long day if he didn't get himself under some kind of control. He lit the fire in the living room, setting the guard round it to prevent Wallace hurting himself, then rescued the kitten from under the tree where he had been intent on ripping as much paper as possible.

'That's enough, *uomo piccolo*,' he murmured. 'Or we'll both be in Hannah's bad books.'

After encouraging Wallace away from the presents and helping Hannah in the kitchen, peeling potatoes and doing other chores, Nic persuaded her to relax by the fire and get round to opening presents.

His eyes widened when he discovered her first gift to him. 'Where did you find it?' he murmured in delight as he looked over the book containing a collection of Stanley Holloway monologues, including

Marriott Edgar's comic rhyme from which Wallace had got his name.

'In a second-hand bookshop near the Castle in Edinburgh.' She smiled. 'Is it the right one?'

'Perfect! Have you read "The Lion and Albert"?'

'I have. And I still think Wally is misnamed!' She laughed, their gazes straying to where the kitten played with rolled-up balls of wrapping paper, purring contentedly.

Nic reached out and took her hand. 'Thank you, Hannah. It means a lot to me to have this. My copy was lost when the house was destroyed in the earthquake.'

'I'm glad you like it,' she whispered, her eyes reflecting her rush of emotions, from sympathy for his loss to awareness of his touch.

Resisting the urge to pull her back into his arms, he pressed a kiss to her palm before releasing her, then handed over his first present to her, a smile curving his mouth at her delighted reaction when she opened it.

'Oh, it's gorgeous!' she exclaimed, studying the hand-crafted silver brooch of a mischievous kitten caught suspended from a branch by its front paws, a comical expression on its face. She pinned it to her top. 'Thank you.'

The rest of their presents, from each other, friends,

staff and the community, left them both with piles of books, CDs and chocolates, and Wallace with far too many treats and new toys. After clearing up the mess of discarded paper and packaging, they had lunch, the mood light and companionable.

'That was amazing,' Nic praised, unable to manage another mouthful of the wonderful fare Hannah had prepared. 'I should never have let you persuade me to have that second piece of pudding.'

Relaxed and flushed, she smiled. 'Perhaps you should go and walk it off while I do the washing-up.'

'No, we will wash up together and then walk together,' he decided, rising to his feet with a groan and giving his full stomach a rueful pat.

It was crisp but sunny when they left the house, walking through the woods at the end of the garden before joining the path that took them behind the village and around the side of the loch. The landscape looked beautiful with its coating of snow, the cold expanse of water backdropped by trees and hills. He stood still for a moment, enjoying the silence, watching a flotilla of wild ducks on the loch, feeling more at peace than he had for a very long time. More and more, Lochanrig was seeping into his blood, his very being.

A cold, wet snowball hit him squarely on the side of the neck, icy liquid trickling uncomfortably down inside the top of his jacket and jumper.

'*Dio!*'

He spun round and managed to duck as Hannah launched a second missile at him. Picking up a handful of snow, he began shaping it as he advanced towards her, smiling as her grin faded and she started stepping backwards. Another second and she turned and ran towards the woods but he caught her easily before she reached the trees and they tumbled down into a soft bank of snow, laughing and gasping for breath. As he held the neck of her jacket back, her hands grasped his arm, eyes wide with a mix of fun and disbelief.

'You wouldn't,' she challenged.

'No?' He teased her a bit longer, allowing a few icy drops to reach her skin, but having her wriggling under him was playing havoc with his self-control. As his awareness and arousal grew, so did Hannah's wary discomfort and, not wanting to spoil this special day, or the happy, relaxed mood, he relented. 'You are right. I am too much of a gentleman!'

Pushing himself off her with reluctance, he rose to his feet and helped her up, keeping hold of her hand as they made their way back to the house, wet, chilly but contented. He helped her off with her jacket, hanging it near the fire to dry.

'Thanks.' She smiled. 'I'm going to pop upstairs and put some dry jeans on.'

Before she went, he caught her to him for a moment, cupping her cool face in his hands and giving her an all too brief kiss. 'Thank you, *cara*, for making this such a special Christmas.'

CHAPTER NINE

HAVING miraculously stayed quiet on Christmas Day, the phone calls came thick and fast in the days ahead and the week sped by. The snow lingered and, while it looked pretty, it made getting to outlying patients in the hills even harder.

'*Dio*, it's cold,' Nic exclaimed as he came in after dark from a call on New Year's Eve. 'You were right about falls from new bicycles. I've dealt with two broken collar-bones and a dislocated shoulder in the last couple of days, not to mention assorted grazes, sprains and a chipped tooth!'

'It's been mad, hasn't it?'

She glanced at Nic as he lay on the settee, Wallace's little paws massaging his chest as the kitten danced up and down, playing with Nic's fingers. How had these two become so much a part of her very existence so quickly? Thanks to Nic, for the first time in many years her Christmas had not been lonely. Now nearly half his time here was over.

Having been desperate to send him away the moment she had realised who he was, she now couldn't bear the thought of him leaving. But she had so many issues to resolve, things she didn't think she could face. And, by his own admission, Nic couldn't put down roots or do commitment. His heart remained with Federica, the woman he had lost his heart to and with whom he had planned a family. Her unsettling thoughts were interrupted by the ringing of the telephone and she groaned as she rose to her feet to answer it.

'Hello, Dr Frost speaking.'

She listened to the information, her nerves jangling, a knot of dread in the pit of her stomach at the summons to the police station. Hanging up the phone a few moments later, she twisted her trembling fingers together and turned to Nic, unable to meet his darkly intent gaze.

'I have to go out.'

'Hannah?' She heard the concern and puzzlement in his voice as he sat up, swinging his feet off the settee and on to the floor. 'Do you want me to do it?'

Yes, she wanted to beg, but couldn't. 'No. It's all right,' she tried to reassure him, her voice edgy.

She pulled on her coat and picked up her bag,

checking she had her keys and mobile phone. Nic came to the door, Wallace cupped gently in one olive-toned hand. Hannah swallowed, her gaze skittering away when she saw the troubled expression in his eyes.

'Hannah?'

'There's a chicken casserole in the oven. You get on with your supper, I might be a while,' she said evasively, walking to the door but wishing she didn't have to face what lay ahead.

'Thanks for coming so quickly,' Sergeant Harris greeted her when she arrived at the police station.

Hannah nodded, tightening her hold on her bag to stop her hands shaking. 'What happened?'

'Young woman on holiday here. She got separated from her friends and was assaulted. She's not been able to tell us much more but she refused to go to hospital so we need you to check her over.'

'Of course. What's her name?'

'Suzanne Smyth.'

Legs like jelly, Hannah followed the gruff but kindly policeman to the small treatment room in the station. The girl was huddled in a chair, a blanket round her shoulders, her clothes torn, her face streaked with mascara from her tears. The breath lodged in Hannah's throat. She found it impossible to stay detached from the victim's distress.

'Hello, Suzanne,' she said with a smile when they were alone, setting her bag down on the desk and taking off her coat. 'I'm Dr Hannah Frost. I've come to see how you are and if there's anything I can do. I need to check you over. Is that OK?'

The tall, thin blonde looked at her through tear-filled hazel eyes. 'I suppose so. I just feel so horrible.'

'I know. Can you tell me what happened?' she asked gently, helping the girl up onto the examination table.

'One moment I was with my friends, the next they'd gone in the crowds. This man, he—'

As Suzanne broke off, sobbing, Hannah did her best to comfort her, despite the emotions churning inside her, the sick dread of fear in her stomach. Slowly the story emerged. It could have been much worse, Hannah knew, but it was bad enough to leave the poor girl bruised and shaken and very frightened.

Hannah felt shaken herself when she finally arrived home from the police station, her examination of Suzanne completed. She had done what she could to advise the girl and had promised to write to her own general practitioner, but it was understandable Suzanne had found it overwhelming. Her fingers shook as she inserted her key in the lock, went inside and closed the front door as quietly as she could, tiptoeing towards the stairs.

'Hannah?' Her heart sank as Nic appeared in the kitchen doorway. 'Is something wrong?'

'No,' she lied.

'I've saved supper for you.'

'I'm not hungry.'

A frown creased his brow. 'You need to eat, *cara*.'

'Not right now.'

'Hannah…'

Setting down her bag, she hung up her coat, aware of the tremor that refused to leave her. She manufactured a feeble smile, unable to hold on much longer. 'I'm very tired. If you'll excuse me, I'm going to have an early night.'

'But—'

'Goodnight, Nic.'

She all but ran up the stairs to her room. Closing the door, she leant back against it, raising her hands to her face and finding her cheeks wet with tears. Slipping off her clothes, she went to the shower, her tears mingling with the spray of water as she scrubbed herself clean. Poor Suzanne. Hannah shivered, struggling to push the thoughts and images away. She pulled on comforting pyjamas, then snuggled down in bed, dragging a spare pillow towards her and hugging it close. She squeezed her eyes shut against the tears, against the memories, but she couldn't banish them.

Not for the first time in her life, she felt scared and unutterably alone…

Nic hesitated outside Hannah's door. The water had run for ages, but now all was silent. He couldn't banish the disquieting feeling that something was very wrong. Softly, he tapped on the door. When there was no answer, he cautiously opened it and stepped inside. The bedside light was on, casting its pale glow across the figure in the bed. Moving forward, he looked down at Hannah, his throat tightening as he saw the way she hugged the pillow—for comfort or protection, he didn't know—her pale cheeks marked by the tracks of tears. He swallowed, his eyes closing briefly, his heart heavy with her pain.

'Hannah?' he whispered. 'Can I sit down?'

No invitation was forthcoming but neither did she reject him when, after a few moments' hesitation, he sat on the edge of the bed as close to her as he dared. The urge to hold her was overwhelming, but he forced himself to resist the temptation. What had happened this evening? Where had she been?

'Talk to me.'

She shook her head, chestnut waves falling across her face, hiding her expression. Reaching out, he gently brushed the strands away and began to stroke her hair. He felt the tremor run through her, couldn't forget the way her hands had been shaking earlier, even before she had gone out.

'Hannah, let me help, please.'

'You can't,' she whispered, her voice throaty.

'How do you know until we try?'

She wiped a hand across her face, smudging the tears. 'I can't.'

'Don't you trust me?' he murmured, moving closer, his hand leaving her hair, his fingers closing around hers.

'It's not that.' She sighed, rolling onto her back but still not meeting his gaze. 'It's not you, Nic.'

He was silent for a few moments, caressing her hand, feeling the erratic dance of her pulse as his fingers strayed over her wrist. 'Where have you been?'

'Just on a difficult call,' she said evasively.

'Who to?'

'No one we know—not a local.' Her gaze, anxious and bruised, slid to his face then away again. 'Why the inquisition?'

'You're surprised I am concerned? You are fine

one moment, get a call that upsets you, go out and come home in tears… How am I meant to react, *cara*?' he questioned, unable to keep an edge of frustration from his voice.

'You don't have to worry about me.'

He saw fresh tears glisten in her eyes and slid his hand to her face, preventing her looking away. 'I can't help but worry. Why is it so hard for you to allow anyone to care or get close? What are you worried I might find out?' he asked huskily, seeing her alarm, feeling her tense.

'Nothing,' she whispered, but he knew it was a lie.

'Move over,' he instructed, releasing her and taking off his boots.

'W-what are you doing?'

Dio, she looked scared. 'I'm not leaving you alone, Hannah, but I think I am a bit warmer and more understanding to hug than a pillow,' he teased, aiming for a lightness he was far from feeling as he took it from her and tucked it behind his head as he slid, fully clothed, into bed beside her.

'But—'

'Nothing's going to happen to you,' he murmured, soothing her. 'Is that what you're frightened of?'

'No.'

He heard her indrawn breath, the rushed denial he

didn't believe, and turned onto his side to look at her. 'Hannah—'

'Don't, Nic. I can't do this. Not tonight. Maybe not ever.'

Aching for the pain that was so evident in her voice, frustrated that he couldn't yet help her, Nic frowned, realising he would get nowhere by pushing further. As had been the way from the beginning with this woman, he had to tread softly and slowly.

'It's OK, *innamorata*.' He shifted on to his back, trying to get more comfortable. 'No more talking. At least have a hug, yes?'

An eternity passed before she moved. Nic found he was holding his breath, knowing how difficult she found this, hoping she wasn't going to reject even the most basic of comforts. He exhaled with a sigh of relief as she finally turned towards him and he wrapped his arms around her, feeling her hesitancy before her arm came to rest over his stomach and she tentatively settled her cheek on his chest. With one hand he brushed the hair back from her face, dropping a kiss on the top of her head.

'Sleep now. I won't let anything happen to you.'

He lay, staring into the darkness, feeling her gradually relax, hearing her breathing change, his mind busy as he wondered what was wrong and how he was going to help her.

Hannah felt confused but incredibly safe. Eyes closed, she struggled from sleep, trying to remember why things felt different, what had happened. As the memories unfolded one by one, she tensed, her lashes slowly rising to assess the situation and find out if the body to which she was pressed was real or some figment of her imagination. Oh, God, it was real!

It was very dark outside and although the bedside lamp cast a muted glow, she couldn't see the clock. What had possessed her to turn into Nic's arms? Yes, he was warmer and more understanding than the pillow she had been cuddling, but he was also infinitely more dangerous. Frightened to move in case she woke him, Hannah took stock. Somehow her legs had ended up tangled with his and, she realised absently, he must be uncomfortable sleeping in all those clothes. His arms were around her, the hand at her waist having somehow found the gap between her pyjama top and bottoms. It rested on her skin, making her burn. One of her arms was thrown across his abdomen, the other trapped underneath her and going numb. She tried unsuccessfully to move it and stifled a whimper of pain.

Carefully, she lifted her head from his chest, easing back to look at his face. Impossibly long lashes fanned lean cheeks and stubble darkened his jaw. Her gaze moved to his mouth. No one should be allowed to look like that. His mouth could tempt a saint. She studied his lips, slightly parted as he slept, remembering how they had felt when he had kissed her, the taste of him. Unconsciously, she licked her own lips. With a sigh her gaze drifted back up his face, a gasp of shock escaping as she found his eyes open, watching her, the expression in them hot and sultry.

'I promised not to touch you,' he whispered, his voice rough, the fingers on her bare back starting to move in a soft, spine-tingling caress. 'So don't look at me like that. My willpower is not infallible.'

Unable to look away, she swallowed. 'What time is it?'

'Four a.m.,' he told her after a brief glimpse at the clock.

'M-my arm's gone to sleep.'

She wriggled, freeing her arm from under her, unintentionally rubbing against him.

'*Arresto*!' he groaned, his hands tightening on her to hold her still. 'Stop.'

'Sorry.'

Her gaze flew back to his face, seeing the faint

flush across his cheekbones, the warmth of desire darkening his eyes.

'Hannah,' he breathed huskily.

Oh, help! One hand locked in the hair at her nape and he drew her head down to his. Unresisting, her eyes fluttered closed, her lips parting to the touch of his. Dear God, the man could kiss. It was like an art form to him, something to be savoured and indulged in, his tongue exploring, teasing and driving her to a delicious frenzy. His hand trailed up her side, slowly moving round to shape the fullness of her breast through the fabric of her top, his thumb stroking over the hardened peak, making her moan, her body arching against him.

He wrenched away, dragging his jumper over his head before reaching for her again, his mouth trailing a hot line of kisses down her throat, the rasp of stubble on her skin making her tingle. One by one, his fingers freed the buttons of her pyjama top before sliding inside, his caresses setting her aflame.

'Nic…'

'Touch me,' he breathed, his teeth nibbling her earlobe.

Uncertain, she tentatively ran her hand across his chest, feeling the thud of his heart beneath his ribs, aware of his warmth, the scent of his skin. She trembled as his mouth inched hotly down towards her breasts. Oh, God, what was she doing? Anxiety had already begun to permeate the fog of pleasure when he rolled them over, his body holding hers down, his hand sliding inside the waistband of her pyjama bottoms. Hannah froze, unable to control her reaction as she instinctively shrank from the intimacy of his touch and fought against the press of his weight.

'Don't hurt me.'

Nic felt as if he had been doused in icy water. He swore under his breath when he saw the fear Hannah could not hide and forced himself to ease away, giving her some space. This never should have happened—wouldn't have happened had he been in proper control of himself. But he had woken up to find Hannah wrapped round him, looking at him as if she returned his desire, and he'd been too impatient, so caught up in his own need for her that he'd forgotten the unresolved issues.

'What is it?' she whispered, looking up at him through huge green eyes as if unaware she had spoken aloud. 'Did I do something wrong?'

Nic gathered her to him, his voice soothing 'No, of course not.'

'Then w-why?'

'Because you're not ready, *innamorata*. When our time comes, it will be because you want it as much as I do, not because you have to steel yourself to go through with it.'

Tears squeezed between her lashes. 'I'm sorry.'

'There's nothing to apologise for,' he admonished, tenderly wiping the wetness from her cheeks. 'Don't cry. Everything will be all right, Hannah, I promise you.'

Cradling her in his arms, careful not to crowd her, he soothed her until she calmed. When at last she was sleeping, he slipped from the bed and went to the shower, stripping off the rest of his clothes and stepping under the stinging cold barbs. He pressed his forehead against the cool tiles, fists clenched, waiting for his white-hot anger to subside. Anger at whoever had done this to her. More of the pieces of the jigsaw puzzle were fitting together and he didn't like the picture it made. He turned his face to the water, trying to drown out the image of Hannah's fear, the sound of her heartfelt plea. Jimmy's words came back to him, the older man's belief that something had happened to Hannah while she had been away from Lochanrig. The lump in his throat threatened to choke him. *Dio*, just how bad had it been?

Shivering, both from the cold and his thoughts, he dried himself and wrapped a towel around his waist. Returning to the bedroom, he gathered up his things, careful not to disturb Hannah's restless sleep as he rescued his jumper and boots from the floor by the bed. He looked down at her for a long moment before moving quietly back to his own room, his mind troubled.

It was light when Hannah next woke and she discovered she was alone. She groaned as jumbled memories flooded back and she rolled over, burying her face in the pillow with an anguished groan. She was so embarrassed. Dear God, how could she ever face him again? Nic must think her the worst kind of tease, leading him so far and then acting like a madwoman and pushing him away.

Somehow she forced herself from the bed and after a quick shower she took her time getting dressed. As she left her room she heard noise and movement downstairs. Nic was in the kitchen. The aroma of percolating coffee filtered tantalisingly to her as she walked down the stairs, her legs unsteady. Trembling with nerves, she pushed open the kitchen door. Nic turned from the counter to smile at her. Wallace was bounding around the floor, playing with a toy mouse.

'Good morning.'

'Morning,' she managed, seeing neither censure nor pity nor amusement in his dark eyes. Just kindness.

'The coffee is ready and there's toast and honey. I was just making myself some scrambled egg. Would you like some?'

She shook her head and sat down before her legs gave way, grateful he was making this as easy as possible. 'You've been busy,' she remarked, looking at the breakfast laid out on the table.

'I'm hungry. I was up early for a call.'

'I didn't hear the phone! I'm sorry, Nic, it was my responsibility to go.'

'Hush, it's OK.' He silenced her with a smile, then his face became serious and her nerves knotted once more. 'I've had to admit Mary McFee to hospital. She has pneumonia.'

Troubled, Hannah set down her knife, her appetite deserting her. 'Poor Mary. I was out there before Christmas and both Shona and Debbie have been in since. What happened?' she asked, concern for the elderly lady pushing all thoughts of her own troubles aside.

'Carole MacLean from the farm said Mary's health worsened a couple of days ago but she refused to allow her to ring us. Carole has been checking Mary regularly and was so worried last night that she decided to look in on her very early when Joe got up for milking. Lucky she did.'

'I'll go in to see her in hospital later today.'

Serving up his scrambled eggs on granary toast, Nic set his plate on the table and sat down opposite her. 'Don't expect too much, *cara.*'

'I suppose I should have pressed for her to go into care,' she mused sadly, blaming herself for allowing things to get to such a state.

'It's not your fault. She was adamant, no, that she would not leave her home?'

'It meant a lot to her to stay there, even though it was totally unsuitable.'

'Then she would have been very unhappy to be moved.' He reached out and briefly covered her hand with his before continuing with his meal. 'You gave her the time she wanted.'

Despite Nic's efforts to ease the tension, Hannah was relieved when a call came in and she insisted on taking it, grateful to get out of the house for a while and put some space between them, although her thoughts weighed heavily on her as she travelled out to a village in their catchment area.

'I'm sure it's appendicitis,' Hannah confirmed a while later, smiling sympathetically at the twelve-year-old girl who lay uncomfortably in bed. She glanced up at the girl's mother. 'We'll need to get Karen to hospital, Mrs Dunlop. Will you and your husband be able to drive her in?'

Mrs Dunlop nodded. 'Yes, thank you, Dr Frost.'

'I'll sit with Karen if you want to make arrangements and pack some things.'

'That would be so kind,' Mrs Dunlop exclaimed gratefully.

'What will happen?' Karen whispered after her mother had gone.

Hannah held the girl's hand. 'They'll examine you and do a few tests, then you'll go to sleep and when you wake up you'll begin to feel very much better.'

'I don't like hospitals.'

Hannah's smile slipped several notches, but she brushed sudden memories of her own experiences aside. 'No, I don't think anyone does, but you'll be home again soon,' she said reassuringly.

Back in her car after the family had set off on the half-hour journey to town, Hannah was about to head home when the beep of her mobile phone announced the arrival of a text message.

'Hannah, Sgt Harris needs to see you about the girl you attended yesterday. Nic.'

Hell and damnation. What exactly had the sergeant told Nic? Anxious, Hannah texted back.

'I'll go there next and then see Mary McFee. H.'

A few moments later the phone beeped again.

'Joanne McStay has just rung, her mama's had a fall. I'm going there now. Nic.'

'OK. H.'

'See you later. Nic.'

That's what worried her, Hannah thought, putting the car in gear.

It was after lunch when she returned to the house but she had not long been in, briefly exchanging details on the progress of Mrs McStay and Mary McFee with Nic, when they were both called out again. Nic went to a tractor accident at a nearby farm while Hannah attended a young child with what turned out to be a case of gastroenteritis, before being called to a car accident on the hill road. By the time she came back it was already seven, Nic was in and, she discovered, had prepared one of his quick but delicious pasta specials.

They talked of their day's cases over the meal and Hannah started to relax, feeling that maybe she had got away with things and Nic hadn't gleaned any unwanted information from Sergeant Harris. By the time Wallace had been fed and the washing-up done, she was looking forward to flopping out in front of the fire. She walked through to the living room and found Nic had apparently had the same idea. He had added more logs and drawn the curtains, and the room felt warm and cosy.

'There's nothing worth watching on TV,' she complained, tossing the paper down on the table.

'Good.'

She glanced at him, curled as he was at one end of the settee, a determined glint in his dark eyes. Silently, his gaze holding hers, he held out his hand. Hannah swallowed. Every instinct told her to run in the opposite direction, so why were her feet closing the distance between them? Confused and nervous, she hesitated, but Nic leant forward and took her hand, drawing her towards him. He shifted sideways on the settee, encouraging her to sit so that she was settled in his arms, her back resting against his chest. Silence stretched and she was painfully conscious of him, aware of his every breath, his scent, his whole being seeming to envelop her, making her feel secure despite her anxiety.

'It's time, Hannah,' he finally told her, stroking her hair.

She didn't pretend not to know what he meant. Instead, she stared into the flames, thankful he had arranged this so she didn't have to face him, a ragged breath escaping as she acknowledged she was not going to be able to evade things this evening. But she didn't know where to start, how to discuss events she had kept hidden for so long, things she had never told another living soul.

Sighing, her head dropped forward. 'I can't do this.'

'Yes, you can. And you're not doing it alone. I'll be here as long as you need me,' he promised, his free hand holding one of hers, fingers entwining.

'Nic…'

'Start with the police station,' he suggested softly. 'You were called to a girl who had been assaulted?'

Hannah nodded, closing her eyes as she remembered Suzanne's distress. 'I just find that kind of thing upsetting.'

'We all do. But you were shaking before you even left here, Hannah. Does it make you remember what happened to you?'

'Sort of,' she whispered.

'You were assaulted?'

'Not like that.'

Nic let out a slow breath. 'These last weeks I've been through the usual lost love, jilted for best friend, found out he was married, and so on, only none of that fits. But someone, at some time, has dented your self-belief that you are a beautiful and desirable woman.'

'That's not it,' she refuted with a frown. 'Not that I think I am beautiful or desirable, I know I'm not. I'm just, I don't know, frigid, I suppose.'

'You most certainly are not,' he corrected huskily with a shocked laugh.

'I don't enjoy it.'

'Sex?'

Dear God, this was awful. Unable to force the words out, she nodded.

'Someone hurt you? Physically?' he questioned, his voice controlled.

Hannah swallowed and nodded again.

'This man hit you?'

'No.' She closed her eyes. 'We had sex. I didn't want to, he—'

'He raped you.'

'It wasn't like that. I wasn't attacked in the street, he wasn't a stranger.'

'Hannah, if you said no and he didn't listen, it's rape,' Nic insisted angrily. 'There is no excuse. Ever. What happened, *cara*?'

Tears trickled down her cheeks as she remembered the awful night her two-year nightmare had begun. 'I'd been seeing this guy from the hospital,' she told him, her voice shaking.

'He was a medical student like you?'

'No, a junior manager. I'd had boyfriends before, but no one I wanted to take things further with,' she explained. 'I hated it in Birmingham but I was desperate to be a doctor, so I kept my head down and worked hard. Then this guy asked me out. He seemed kind, easy to talk to, I liked him. We went out, kissed a few times but I didn't feel anything, not like that, you know? He was just a friend, or so I thought.'

'I understand. What happened then?' Nic prompted, his thumb stroking distracting caresses around her palm.

'There was a party for Bonfire Night and he asked me to go. I wasn't that keen but I agreed. We hadn't been there long when I started to feel strange. I thought he was being kind when he said he'd take me home but he had planned it all, had drugged my wine. Indoors, he turned on me, said I owed it to him. I tried to say n-no, that I didn't want to, but I couldn't move or speak. He wouldn't s-stop.' She shivered, tears stinging her eyes, and Nic's arms tightened round her. 'I was so scared. He was really heavy, holding me down. I thought he was going to smother me. Outside fireworks were going off, people were laughing, but I couldn't call anyone. I'd never done it before. It was horrible. It really hurt.'

Nic swore in Italian, sounding shocked and furious. 'Oh, Hannah,' he whispered against her ear, his warm breath fanning her skin.

'It wasn't until the next day, when whatever he gave me was wearing off, that I realised he hadn't used anything and I was terrified I might get pregnant.'

'And did you?'

Hannah shook her head, her fingers tightening on his. 'No. And subsequent HIV-AIDS tests were clear. For a while I thought I was physically OK,' she added, feeling him stiffen as he took on board what she said.

'But you weren't?' he murmured, his voice rough.

'No. That was just the beginning.'

She felt Nic's tension. 'Hannah?'

'I started getting terrible pains, feeling ill. One day I collapsed. He'd given me chlamydia, but it was incorrectly treated with the wrong antibiotics and I developed a serious pelvic infection.'

'*Maledizione*!' Nic breathed, his fingers gentle as he brushed the tears from her face.

'I went to a gynae specialist at a different hospital,' she continued in a rush, unable to stop now she had started. 'The pain was so bad I couldn't work and nothing was helping. I was told that I was probably infertile, that I may never have a family of my own. Not that I was ever going to love anyone or have a relationship after that.'

She heard Nic's indrawn breath, then he moved, turning them so he could gather her close but see her face. Her gaze met his and she saw the sympathy and shock and hurt in his dark eyes, the glisten of moisture he made no attempt to hide.

'What you went through was criminal,' he told her, his voice raw with emotion. 'Did you not tell anyone?'

'I couldn't.'

'Not even your parents?'

'Especially not them. They would have been so disappointed in me.'

He looked down at her, a frown on his face. 'None of this was your fault, *cara*. You do know that, don't you?'

'I suppose,' she murmured uncertainly, seeing his frown deepen.

'It wasn't, Hannah,' he insisted, pausing for a few moments before he continued. 'So when you recovered, you decided sex must always be like that, that there was something wrong with you?'

Hannah nodded. 'I just remember the fear and the pain.'

'So work only for the rest of your life?'

'I wanted to come back here, where it was safe, and be a GP. I never met anyone, never wanted to, you know—' She snapped off the words, just managing to stop herself from saying 'until you'.

'And you really believe you have no sexual feelings?' he asked incredulously.

'I just don't feel anything.'

His fingers under her chin tilted her face up and she saw the mischievous twinkle light his eyes. 'Really? You feel nothing when I touch you?' he asked softly.

'Nic, I…'

Her words trailed off as he ran his fingers tantalisingly over her face, leaving every millimetre tingling before brushing across the curve of her lips and slipping his thumb between them when her mouth opened on a gasp.

'You feel nothing when I kiss you?' he teased, replacing his fingers with his lips.

Instantly fire licked through her and her lips parted further in welcome. Her pulse raced as he accepted the invitation, deepening the contact, kissing her with a sensual thoroughness that left her breathless and trembling all over. Helplessly she found herself pressing closer to him, a moan of protest drawn from her when he eased away.

'You still think you don't feel anything?' he murmured huskily, eyes nearly black with passion, a smile curving his far too sexy mouth.

Hannah felt a flush warm her cheeks. She didn't know what to think. Only that with Nic she felt things she had never felt before. As he cupped her face in his hands, his words turned her insides to jelly and brought a rush of fearful anticipation flooding through her.

'Don't worry, Hannah. When the time is right, I'm going to show you how beautiful making love can be.'

CHAPTER TEN

HANNAH was on tenterhooks as the days passed, the combination of fearful anticipation and nervous excitement fuelling her growing skittishness. Part of her was terrified of the day when Nic suggested making good his promise…part of her was inexplicably scared that he wouldn't. Talking to him about what had happened to her had been traumatic but had left her feeling calmer, as if some ghosts had been laid to rest at last.

Of course she didn't want him to make love to her! Did she? No, absolutely not, she told herself, but her resolve seemed shamefully weak, her words hollow ones, especially when even thinking about his touch made her flesh prickle with excitement. As for his kisses… Her eyes closed. Those deep, sensual, consuming kisses that took her breath away. He hadn't kissed her since that night yet she could still taste him, ached to do so again, and—

'Hannah!'

Kirsty's admonition startled her from her thoughts. Her eyes jerked open and she looked up, realising all the practice staff were gathered around the table, staring at her. 'I'm sorry,' she murmured, clearing her throat, trying to banish her sinful thoughts.

'Are you all right?' Kirsty frowned. 'You've been behaving very oddly lately.'

'I'm fine.'

Her gaze skittered down the table to where Nic was sitting and she saw him raise his coffee-mug to his lips to hide his smile. Dark eyes laughed at her. Dear God, he knew, damn him! He knew he was driving her so mad with confusion and expectation that she couldn't think straight any more.

Annoyed, she sat up straight and pulled her notebook towards her. 'Right, let's get on shall we?'

'That's what I said five minutes ago.' Kirsty sighed, shaking her head.

Hannah forced herself to concentrate as they worked through the agenda for the practice meeting, everyone contributing ideas and comments from patient care to general operational issues.

'You all know that Mary McFee was taken ill. I want to thank you all, especially Shona and Debbie, for your hard work caring for her. She's holding her own in hospital but is still very sick and it is unlikely she will go home if she does recover.'

There was general comment and discussion, and Hannah knew how sorry all the staff were in such cases.

'Any news of Mrs McStay?' Shona asked.

Hannah kept her gaze studiously averted as Nic filled them in on the latest update.

'She suffered a complicated break to her arm when she fell but it is mending slowly,' he informed them. 'However, her confusion has worsened considerably and she scarcely recognises Joanne now. I think Joanne knows it is impossible for her to provide the continuing level of help at home that her mother needs. I'm seeing her this week and will suggest the time is right to allow her mother to be moved to somewhere nearby where she can have twenty-four-hour specialist care.'

'I'm sure that's the right thing,' Debbie said, and everyone murmured agreement.

'It's very sad,' Morag sighed. 'Joanne's done such a good job.'

Nic nodded. 'She has, and it is sad, but Joanne is a young woman herself and has to think about her own well-being. I think we need to consider both their needs in helping her reach a decision.'

Hannah silently agreed with Nic's assessment, knowing how much time and effort he had put into the McStays' case and what a difference he had made to Joanne's outlook from that first meeting back in October.

'OK,' she said, moving on to the final subject on her list. 'One of the local practices that share out-of-hours cover have confirmed they are withdrawing their service, as the contract allows them to do.'

Kirsty tutted in disapproval. 'Well, that's going to cause a lot of difficulty, isn't it?'

'It might,' Hannah admitted.

Jane held up her hand. 'You'll be the one affected, Hannah. You're the one called out at nights and weekends. How do you feel?'

'In my experience, the vast majority of patients do not abuse out-of-hours calls,' she began, looking round at her colleagues. 'I'm very uneasy about the new system and I want to provide a continuity of care to our patients. If the other practices did pull out, it would release us from covering their lists and perhaps we could manage our own.' She tried not to glance at Nic as she continued, her voice faltering. 'Of course, it depends on the agreement of whoever else is working here as second doctor.'

She felt Nic's gaze on her but made a pretence of

writing some notes on her pad. The thought of him leaving in a matter of weeks filled her with a cold knot of despair she really didn't want to examine.

'I have something I'd like to put forward,' Kirsty announced.

Hannah dragged her thoughts back to matters at hand and forced a smile. 'Of course.'

'It's not that long before we have to start thinking about a replacement for Nic. Finding the right locum is never easy, nor is it the most satisfactory solution for the patients. That continuity of care, Hannah,' Kirsty stressed.

'I agree,' Morag chipped in.

Hannah frowned. 'So what are you suggesting?'

'We all know why the decision was made to use locums at the time your father died. It was all too much,' Morag said with a sympathetic smile. 'But three and a half years on, maybe it is time to think about taking on a new permanent partner.'

'I see.'

Taken aback by the turn of the conversation, Hannah wondered how long her staff had been thinking this way and why no one had said anything before. She could see the sense of the argument. Her gaze strayed round the table, seeing the general agreement amongst the rest of the staff, although Nic was staring down at his pad, a frown on his face as he twisted his pen through his fingers. Hannah swallowed again, unable to imagine him not being here.

'It probably would be the best idea.' She cleared her throat, trying to ease the sudden roughness from her voice. 'Any feedback from patients, Kirsty?'

'From the comments I get, people would prefer not to have someone new coming and going every few months.'

'I've heard the same,' Jane confirmed.

Manufacturing a smile, Hannah began gathering her things. 'Right. Let me know if you have any more thoughts. Thanks, that's it for this morning.'

A few days later, Nic paused in the doorway of Hannah's consulting room, watching as she frowned down at something she was writing, the tip of her tongue peeping out between her lips. A rush of desire washed over him. He'd wanted to give her some time to come to terms with everything, but the wait was driving him insane. Learning about her past had been a shock and he ached for all she had been through. He wanted to track down the bastard who had caused her so much fear and pain, and take him apart piece by piece. Most of all he longed to do all he could to ease her out of the prison in which she had shut herself for too long. When she glanced up and saw him, he guarded his thoughts and stepped forward.

'Hi.'

'Hello,' she responded with a nervy smile, faint colour staining her cheeks, her eyes revealing her emotions, her confusion and her own flash of desire as her gaze involuntarily dropped to his mouth.

'What were you frowning over?'

Her brow puckered and she looked down at her desk. 'I'm trying to draft out an advertisement for Kirsty to place for a new permanent doctor for the practice,' she admitted, her voice uncharacteristically flat.

'You've decided, then?' he prompted, ignoring the knot in his stomach.

'It's what everyone seems to want.'

'And what do you want?'

Her gaze darkened as she looked up at him, making his pulse race. 'I, um, think it's the best thing to do. You wanted to see me?' she said, after a tense pause.

'Yes.' He struggled to draw his mind back to why he was here. 'I thought you'd like to know that I've had a letter this morning from the endocrinologist about the young man with gynaecomastia.'

Her smile became more natural. 'That's good. What's the news?'

'They'll be doing surgery,' he told her, sitting on the edge of her desk, noting how she clenched her hands together as if preventing herself reaching out to touch his fingers, which rested a few inches away.

'Right. I hope it's a success.'

He rose to his feet, edgy with tension and unfulfilled yearning. 'I'll leave you to get on.'

'Thanks.'

'Hannah…about your advertisement.'

Her eyes widened. 'Yes?'

'Don't forget to say they should be female!' he teased.

As fresh colour washed her cheeks, Nic went back to his own consulting room, his thoughts on Hannah. The time was flying by, he had only a few more weeks here. Frowning, he chased away the unsettling and alarming thoughts that started to nibble at the edges of his mind. The fact was, they didn't have too many more days—or nights—to waste.

Sitting on the rug in front of the fire that night, Hannah played with Wallace, trying to work out why she was so on edge. Nic had been quiet all evening, although when they had been preparing a meal earlier, he had brushed against her or elicited contact between them far more than usual, until she had been at screaming point. And with him dressed in his most disreputable, figure-hugging jeans and a black shirt that he seemed to have forgotten to button properly, her nerves were frayed.

Several times she had felt his gaze on her, but whenever she had looked round, he'd either been napping or reading a book. Was it just her wayward imagination playing tricks on her? It must be, because he seemed relaxed and unconcerned. As if aware he was the object of her thoughts, he closed his book and smiled, rising to his feet with a yawn, stretching in a sinuous way that drew her attention to the lithe perfection of his body.

This was ridiculous, she chastised herself, focusing her attention back on the sleepy kitten. From beneath her lashes she watched as Nic gathered up their empty coffee-mugs and went out to the kitchen, returning a few moments later and leaning in the doorway, looking at her. She glanced up, unnerved by the lazy speculation in his dark eyes.

'Having an early night?' she asked, anticipating some quiet time on her own.

'That's the plan.' He smiled, pushing away from the door. *'E siete venendo con me.'*

'What does that mean?' Damn him, he knew how much that irritated her.

'You really want to know?' he teased, whisking Wallace away to the kitchen.

'Nic, stop being annoying. What did you say?'

She thought he wasn't going to answer as there was a long silence before he surprised her by returning to the living room and walking slowly across to her. *'E siete venendo con me.'* He took her hand, drawing her to her feet.

'What are you doing?' She was unaccountably anxious, her stomach feeling as if it harboured a whole flight of butterflies carrying out acrobatic manoeuvres.

'You asked if I was having an early night,' he reminded her.

'I know.' Her heart started thudding. 'Y-you said yes.'

He gave her hand a gentle tug and started to lead her from the room. 'Then I said, "And you're coming with me."'

Oh, God! At the foot of the stairs she hesitated. 'You're not serious?'

'We're wasting too much time.'

He started up the stairs and, like a lamb to the slaughter, her heart hammering in her chest, she followed. She was trembling from head to foot as Nic led her inexorably to his bedroom.

'This is a bad idea,' she whispered, scarcely able to force the words out.

'You think too much,' he chastised softly. 'You look for problems where there need be none.'

He'd planned this deliberately so she wouldn't have time to worry, she realised. She looked at him, her breath locking in her throat. For years she had avoided this kind of intimacy, tortured by what had happened before, but in a few short weeks Nic had dismantled all her barriers until she now stood before him, on the brink of the most frightening and risky act of her life, her defences in tatters.

A tremble rippled through her as Nic pulled the pins from her hair, releasing the restraining knot so that the chestnut waves fell in a curtain around her shoulders. Cupping her face in his hands, he brushed his lips across hers, increasing the shiver that already ran along her spine.

'We're going to take our time, Hannah, and nothing will happen that you do not want. This I promise you.'

Many times he had told her and shown her how much he wanted her but no matter how aroused he was, or how capricious and beyond his understanding her behaviour, he had always let her go at once if she had said no. She bit her lip, drowning in the dark depths of his eyes.

'Nic…'

'Hush.' Turning, he picked up a shirt and handed it to her, giving her a gentle push towards the bathroom. 'Go. Put this on.'

Legs unsteady, she made it to the *en suite* and closed the door, leaning back against it for support. She held the shirt to her face, her eyes closing as she breathed in the lingering scent of him from the silken fabric. He'd known it would be too much for her to undress in front of him. Grateful for his sensitivity, but still scared, she started to take off her clothes in the privacy of the bathroom, her fingers shaking over the task. They fumbled even more as she drew his shirt over her bare skin, its touch making her tingle. Soon it would be his hands. She sucked in a breath. Slowly she did up the buttons. Now she had to walk back out there. Somehow.

She forced herself to open the door. The bedroom curtains had been drawn, the lights were out and candlelight flickered. The fire had obviously been set some time earlier as it exuded a gentle heat. The room looked cosy, warm…safe. Then her gaze strayed to the bed and she knew it wasn't safe at all. Nic waited for her. His clothes were draped on a nearby chair and it didn't take a genius to work out that he had very little, if anything, left on. Hannah's gaze flicked to where he lay under the covers, just part of his bare chest and his arms on view. Even that brief sight of his olive-toned skin drawn supply over muscle was enough to make her catch her breath.

He held out his hand to her. 'Come here, *innamorata*,' he instructed huskily.

Nervous, she moved forward. It seemed a ridiculously long way. Finally she stood beside the bed, her fingers feeling cool and unsteady as they were entwined with the warmth and strength of his. He partly drew back the duvet and she sat down, sliding her legs underneath before lying on her back, drawing the duvet up to her chin and staring straight up at the ceiling. Oh, God, what was she doing here?

Lying on his side, he watched her. He was still holding her hand, his fingers straying across her palm and over her wrist. Surely he must feel the race of her pulse. Her heart was thudding. The heat of him seeped into her. His scent teased her. Gently he encouraged her onto her side so she had to face him. One finger trailed a line of fire across her cheekbones, her eyes, her jaw line, her mouth. Her gaze met his and she saw the mix of emotions in his eyes, tenderness, understanding, passionate intent.

'Nic, I—'

'Don't be frightened, *cara*,' he gentled, voice husky. 'I'll look after you.'

She felt his breath fan her skin as he rained butterfly kisses over her face, the line of her freckles, her eyelids and then her mouth, teasing her with soft caresses. Hannah gasped as his tongue flicked out to trace her lips. He took advantage of her action, gradually deepening the kiss, sensually sucking on her lower lip before releasing it. Gently he nibbled round her mouth, driving her crazy. She could feel him smile, then his lips settled back over hers, cajoling, seductive, teasingly sliding his tongue lightly into her mouth. She heard her own whimper of desire, was unable to control her response as she kissed him back, involuntarily pressing closer to him. Nic took what she offered, kissing her with such intensity she didn't think she could stand it.

He drew her hand against him, holding her palm on his chest. Hannah revelled in the texture of his warm, hair-brushed skin and ripple of muscle beneath, allowing him to guide her hand slowly over him until she was confident enough to explore on her own, enjoying the way his body responded, his breath shortening, his heart thudding as she ran her fingers over the smooth solidness of his shoulders, his back and round to the breadth of his chest. She hesitated, too nervous and uncertain to go lower.

After what seemed an eternity, when she wanted to cry with frustration, he began touching her through the silken softness of the shirt, fingers working slowly down her spine before journeying back up her side, his thumb brushing the rounded curve of her breast. Hannah moaned against his kiss as he cupped her, filling his hand, shaping her. She protested when he drew back, opening her eyes to find his sultry and dark with passion before he bent his head, closing his mouth over one swollen, hardened nipple. Hannah cried out as his tongue rasped the dampened fabric across her sensitised flesh, her fingers tightening on him.

'Oh, God,' she murmured.

'You like that?'

'Y-yes.'

She arched to him as he did it again. And more. When his hand travelled down below the hem of the shirt, teasing over her bare thigh, she trembled. His fingers inched upwards, exploring the rounded swell of her rear, drawing her towards him, making her all too aware of his own arousal. Gradually his touch became more insistent and intimate as he eased one of her thighs over his and leaned in to her. Feeling more of his weight and the caress of his fingers, Hannah couldn't prevent herself from tensing, or hold back the whimper of alarm that escaped from her.

'Nic?'

'*Prendalo facile,*' he whispered. 'Easy, Hannah.'

As his words silenced her fears, he rolled onto his back, taking her with him, holding her close and kissing her until her arousal built once more. Easing her up to give himself room, his hands slid up under her shirt, caressing her, before moving round to slowly undo the buttons, opening her to him. She shivered as he tossed the garment aside and his fingers returned to trace her skin.

'You're so beautiful.'

Despite her doubts, he made her feel it. Her hands closed on the strength of his shoulders to steady herself as his mouth pleasured first one breast and then the other. She felt the tension in him, the restraint, saw the desire in his eyes he was trying to control. Sensitised to his touch, her own need burned through her, an ache of emptiness inside making her squirm against him, and his hands slid to her hips, moving her, letting her feel all of him.

'Please, Nic,' she whimpered, suffused with heat and unimaginable need.

'This is for you,' he promised, his voice rough, his breath ragged. 'Whatever you want. You're in control.'

She looked down at him, seeing the flush of passion on his face, knowing he was holding back to make this right for her. Brushing the fall of hair back from her face, he drew her head down for his kiss. Oh, God, she wanted him, Hannah acknowledged. Wanted to know what it might be like with him. Fighting her fears, she moved to accept him, hesitant at first, awkward, tense as she expected pain, gradually relaxing as she found none.

Nic helped her, his eyes closing, the breath catching in his throat as they were finally joined, completely, intimately. He thought he had forgotten how to breathe as she slowly and tentatively started to move on him. Keeping still was going to kill him. He opened his eyes, feasting on the sight of her, flushed with passion, lips parted, her beautiful breasts swollen from his caresses, the creamy smoothness of her thighs as she straddled him, her movements becoming less controlled and more urgent.

Unable to bear any distance between them, he ran his hands over her, one locking in the tangle of her hair, urging her down for his kiss. Her breasts pressed against his chest as he loved her mouth, his tongue mimicking what he wished to do to her. With his other hand he explored their joined bodies, unable to prevent himself moving, her moans of pleasure as her time neared exciting him. He fought desperately to keep control so this would be right for her, his heart pounding beneath his ribs as she went over the edge, crying out his name, and he let go, joining her in release. He held her as tears slid between her lashes, falling with her as her body spasmed deliciously around him.

Shaking, she lay on top of him, too shocked and amazed to move. His caresses gentled her, his whispered words in Italian soothing her. He eased them apart, moving her so she was lying more comfortably in his arms, cradling her head against him, wiping away her tears. She heard his breathing slow, his heartbeat calm.

'Thank you,' she whispered when she could manage to speak.

He stroked her with exquisite tenderness. 'Thank you, Hannah.'

'I'm sorry.'

'Excuse me?' He frowned.

'If it wasn't much good for you.'

He tilted her face up to look at her. 'You are joking, yes? Hannah, this was one of the most special experiences of my life,' he insisted, sincerity ringing in his words, warming her.

'I didn't know. That it could be like that, I mean.'

'There is much you still don't know,' he teased, smiling as she flushed. 'But there will be time.'

The husky promise made her shiver with anticipation. 'Nic, I—'

'Still,' he interrupted, lying back, his gaze mischievous. 'It is nothing to get bothered about. Just a mechanical act of procreation, no? Is that not right, *innamorata*?'

Laughter bubbled inside her as he cheekily quoted her words back at her. 'OK, so I might have been wrong.'

'Might have been?' he demanded with mock outrage.

'Perhaps I need a bit more practice to be certain,' she dared to whisper, her breath catching at the look on his face.

'You can have all the practice you want.'

His eyes darkened with desire as his hand slid across her face and into her hair, drawing her closer, his tongue tip tracing the outline of her lips, making her gasp. Dear God, how could she want him again so badly so soon?

'Nic,' she begged, as his mouth continued to tease hers. 'Please.'

Molten dark eyes watched her. 'Do you trust me?'

'Yes'

Hannah spoke without hesitation, knowing it was true. She trusted this man implicitly, as she had trusted no one else before. And, she realised, pushing thoughts of the future away, as she would never trust anyone else again. Knowing their time would be short, that he would be leaving, she didn't want to waste another minute. Holding his gaze, she rolled onto her back, inviting him to follow, to show her everything making love with him could be like.

'Are you sure?' he whispered hoarsely.

Nervous but excited, she nodded. 'Very sure.'

The passion she unleashed took her breath away as Nic's mouth and hands began a lingering exploration of her body that left her quivering with need. She bit her lip, her fingers sinking into his hair when his lips trailed lovingly over her belly. Then her eyes widened in shock as, instead of moving back up as she expected, his lips and fingers explored lower. He couldn't... Oh, God! The breath hissed from her lungs, her body instinctively arching to his touch as he took her to levels of pleasure she had never imagined existed. Just when she thought she couldn't bear it any more, he slid sensually back up her body, his hot, dark gaze holding hers as he joined them with one smooth, sure motion, driving her mad by pausing.

'Am I hurting you?' he whispered.

'No, no.' Her hands slid down his back, her hips moving under his, her legs wrapping round him. 'Don't stop. Please, don't stop.'

Groaning her name, he began to move, taking her on a wild ride that nothing could have prepared her for, leaving her, finally, panting and gasping, washed up entwined with him in some distant, foreign place she had never visited before.

'Hannah, are you all right?'

His husky words permeated the sensual cloud that enveloped her and she nodded. 'I'm fine.' Fine? What a ridiculously insipid word to describe how wonderful and incredible and amazed she felt.

She opened her eyes, seeing the concern in his change to amusement as she gave him a slow smile of utter contentment.

'I feel like a shameless hussy,' she whispered as he gathered her to him, moving so she lay in his arms with her head on his chest.

'Good.' She felt a chuckle rumble inside him. 'Hold that thought!'

Smiling, spent, Hannah closed her eyes, listening to the thud of his heart, feeling the rise and fall of his chest gradually begin to slow. Her smile faded as an aftermath of thoughts began to intrude. Constrained by the ghosts of her past, she had wasted so much time. Weeks of being with Nic had slipped by and now, when she had been given a taste of paradise, in all too short a time it would be snatched away from her again.

Hannah stifled a sob. Nic's touch had healed the painful wounds of her past, had opened her mind, her heart and her body, but soon he would go, and where did that leave her? With nothing. Tonight had worked because Nic was special…compassionate, generous, loving and, oh, so sexy. The spark had been firing between them from the first moment they had met and over the weeks she had fallen in love with him. The reality hit home with painful clarity. What a stupid thing to do. Only heartbreak lay ahead. Because Nic would be leaving. He had told her himself that he didn't do commitment, didn't put down roots.

I'll stay as long as you need me, he had promised. Only he wouldn't, would he? Not beyond his contract. Not for ever. And she was very much afraid that he had come to mean so much to her that even for ever would not be long enough.

Nic lay awake for a long time, savouring the reality of being able to hold her, in his bed, skin on skin. *Dio*, she was so responsive, like a new flower opening in welcome to the sun. He'd never experienced anything so perfect or intense in his life, learning all the places she was most sensitive, where his lightest touch made her squirm with need, hearing her call his name at the height of her pleasure, knowing she had never felt that before.

The knowledge that she had awakened to him but would one day move on after he left brought a searing pain to his chest. He couldn't bear to think of another man touching her. Closing his eyes, he steeled himself to face the fact that they had an agreement and he had to walk away from her when his contract was over.

CHAPTER ELEVEN

'JUST be adult about it,' Hannah lectured her reflection in the mirror. 'You went into this knowing Nic was going to leave.'

It didn't make her feel any better. Neither did it stop the days marching by at an alarming rate. The nights, too. She closed her eyes, thinking of the nights in Nic's bed, a flush warming her cheeks at the memories of the things they had done. Continued to do. Not that it made the slightest difference in terms of easing the desperation of wanting him. If anything, it just fuelled the fire of passion between them. Hannah closed her hands over the side of the vanity unit for support. How could she give him up? They were halfway through February and next month he would walk out of her life for ever. And she couldn't hold him, couldn't beg him to stay, even if he would, because she couldn't give him what he needed, the family he so desperately wanted and had planned with Federica, the woman he still mourned.

'Hannah? We're going to be late.'

Nic's reminder floated up the stairs. 'I won't be a minute,' she called back, putting finishing touches to her appearance.

She wished they didn't have to go but Jane's Valentine's Day wedding was a long-planned event and she knew the young receptionist would be disappointed if they didn't attend the reception as promised. With a sigh, she picked up her bag and went downstairs.

'*Dio!*'

Nic's exclamation hissed out on a whisper of breath as she walked into the kitchen.

'What's wrong?'

'Nothing,' he denied, but she saw his Adam's apple bob as he swallowed, his gaze fixed on her.

'Nic?'

'I thought the jeans were bad.'

'What are you talking about?' She frowned at him.

'I've never seen you in a dress.'

Hannah looked down at her emerald green, above-the-knee dress. 'Is something wrong with it?'

'Yes.'

'I don't understand.'

Smiling, he sat down on a kitchen chair and drew her towards him. 'You look fantastic and you're driving me mad.' His hands slid down to the hem of her skirt and slipped underneath to glide over her thighs, above the tops of her stockings.

'Oh, God,' she breathed, her hands on his shoulders steadying her as her legs turned to jelly, an ache of desire knotting inside her. 'Nic...'

He stood up, holding her against him. 'Feel what you do to me?' he whispered hoarsely.

Hannah shivered at the touch of his hands on her, the evidence of his arousal, her eyes widening as she heard the faint hiss of the zip as he unfastened his trousers.

'We can't!'

'We can.'

He kissed her until she was reeling, dispensing with her panties, his fingers finding her ready for him despite her half-hearted arguments to the contrary. Smiling, he drew up her skirt and backed her up to the kitchen table.

'You said we were late,' she reminded him breathlessly.

'So we'll be late.'

'But—'

He grinned wickedly at her. 'We'll tell them something came up!'

'Oh, God,' she sighed again, her feverish gaze

locked with his as she wrapped her legs around his hips in encouragement and welcomed him inside her.

They were late. Hannah felt she must have a neon sign flashing over her head, telling everyone what they had been doing, as she mumbled her apologies to Jane's family.

'An unexpected emergency,' Nic explained smoothly, laughter in his eyes as colour washed her cheeks.

They helped themselves to food from the buffet and circulated, Hannah trying to keep some distance between her and Nic, fearful she would give something away or disgrace herself. The man only had to look at her and she wanted him.

'Jane looks happy,' Nic murmured in her ear, and she started, taking a step away.

'Yes, she does.' She watched the young woman and her new husband, in full Scottish dress, canoodling before they cut the cake. 'So does Craig.'

'I'd never make a Scotsman—I hate whisky and I won't wear a kilt!'

'Not even for me?' she teased.

His eyes turned sultry and he leaned over to whisper in her ear. 'Maybe in the privacy of our bedroom, *innamorata*!'

'Nic, stop it!'

'How long do we have to stay here?'

Hannah glanced at him and grinned. 'Hours, I expect.'

'Don't,' he groaned. 'I can't wait that long.'

'Behave yourself.'

'It's your fault for wearing that dress,' he complained, his voice rough.

Warmed by his desire for her, Hannah forced herself to move away and chat to some of the other guests, not wanting to draw attention to her and Nic.

'How's it going, Doc?' Allan Pollock said, the jovial garage owner attending the reception with his wife, Dorothy.

'Fine.' Hannah smiled. 'How are you both?'

'Not so bad, Doc. The old knee's holding up. I did what you said and saw your physio for the exercises.'

'When I remind him to do them,' Dorothy added with an indulgent smile.

Hannah laughed. 'Well, you keep nagging him, Dorothy. And come back any time, Allan, if you're having problems.'

'Will do, Doc, thanks.' He paused, his gaze straying around the room. 'Shame Dr Nic will be moving on. He's settled in so well here, everyone likes him.'

'Yes,' Hannah managed, not wanting to be reminded of the fast-approaching day when Nic would leave.

'Aye, well, I'm sure you'll do your best to get someone as good.' Allan smiled before he and Dorothy were hailed by other friends and turned away.

'That won't be easy, will it?'

Hannah spun round at the sound of Kirsty's voice. 'You made me jump!'

'Sorry.' The older woman smiled. 'I overheard what Allan said and it won't be easy to replace Nic.'

'We always manage somehow,' Hannah pointed out, unwilling to be drawn, shifting uncomfortably under Kirsty's probing gaze.

'We'll see what the applicants are like when you start interviewing.'

'Indeed.' She glanced around for an escape and saw Jane smile and wave at her. Smothering her relief, Hannah turned back to Kirsty. 'Excuse me, I must have a quick word with Jane.'

She was halfway across the room when she felt a hand tap insistently on her arm and she looked down, recognising Debbie's seven-year-old daughter.

'Hi, Kim,' she said.

The girl pressed a set of keys into her hand. 'Dr Nic says can you get his bag from the car and go into the next room without letting everyone know there's a problem?' the girl repeated solemnly.

'Yes, of course.' Hannah ran a comforting hand over the child's dark hair. 'You all right?'

'I'm OK.'

'Good girl.'

'I've got to get Mummy now,' she said, heading off into the throng of wedding guests.

Concerned, Hannah collected Nic's medical bag from the boot of his car and hurried to the adjoining room.

'What's happened?' she asked quietly, finding Nic attending a woman who was sitting on one of the chairs. 'Oh, no, it's Patricia, Jane's mother.'

Nic grimaced, opening his bag to find his stethoscope and sphygmomanometer to take Patricia's blood pressure, wrapping the cuff around her arm, frowning as he recorded the measurement.

Hannah sat down, taking Patricia's hand in hers. 'I know it's scary, but try not to worry.' She smiled, suspecting a transient ischaemic attack, or mini-stroke. The woman seemed to be able to hear what was going on around her but had lost her speech.

'I saw her come in here and thought she looked strange,' Nic explained, taking off his stethoscope after listening to her heart. 'I decided to see if she was OK. She was very slurred, said she was dizzy, and then slumped over and couldn't talk. I've called an ambulance on my mobile and Debbie has gone to talk to Jane and her father.'

'It was lucky you were so alert.'

The next ten minutes were chaotic as Jane and her father came rushing in with Debbie, Craig close behind them, all understandably distraught at what had happened. While Nic concentrated on caring for Patricia, Hannah explained things to the worried family.

'We'll get her off to hospital and she'll be thoroughly checked out,' Hannah told them gently. 'I know it's very frightening but there is a good chance she'll be fine. The doctors will assess the problem, what might have caused it and what the extent of it is. It doesn't mean she will have a full stroke, OK? They'll advise on medications necessary and any future monitoring.'

Brian Thompson nodded and Jane held tightly to Craig's hand, tears glistening on her lashes. Hannah was relieved when the ambulance arrived and Patricia was safely on her way to Casualty, the family following behind.

'Hospital first?' Nic asked when they climbed into his car a short while later.

'Do you mind?'

His smile was wry. 'Of course not. I'm worried

about them, too. Just keep your coat on,' he added as a teasing aside, lightening the subdued atmosphere.

Hannah smiled back, grateful for his compassion and his humour. Allan and Kirsty were right. It would be impossible to find another doctor with Nic's special qualities.

'You got off on honeymoon all right in the end, then?' Hannah said with a smile when Jane came back to work two weeks later.

'We did. A couple of days' delay, but it was fine. Thanks to you and Nic,' she added. 'Mum's doing really well and her speech is much better than it was.'

Hannah placed a hand on her arm. 'I'm so glad, Jane, but it's Nic you really need to thank.'

'I'll see him now, before the rush starts,' the young woman said, heading off to his consulting room.

Hannah herself scarcely saw Nic all day as they were both kept busy with surgeries, clinics and home visits. She was in the kitchen, preparing a meal, when she heard him come home, greeting an ever-more adventurous and growing Wallace in the hallway. She smiled as she heard him talking to the little cat, a shiver running through her when his footsteps approached behind her as she stood at the sink. His arms slid round her and she leant back against him as he kissed her neck, nipping the lobe of her ear. She held onto the sink, her legs feeling shaky as he pressed against her, letting her know how much he wanted her. Again. And, God help her, she wanted him, too.

Wriggling round, hands wet, she wrapped her arms around his neck, meeting and matching the hot intensity of his kiss. She wasn't sure who moaned loudest in protest when the telephone rang, but she dragged herself away from him reluctantly, not entirely steady on her feet as she went to answer it.

'What?' he sighed when she came back a few moments later.

'I'm sorry, I'm on BASICS call tonight. I have to go.'

'I know.' He cupped her face and dropped a kiss on her lips. 'Where is it?'

'The motorway.' She grimaced, struggling into her things as he collected her bag for her.

'You take care. Please, *cara*.'

'I will. It sounds like a bad one, though, so don't wait up.'

Much to her despair, her predictions came true, and it was nearly midnight by the time she arrived home, having been stuck at the scene of the multiple pile-up in fog for hours. Fortunately no one had lost their lives but several people had serious injuries. After locking up, she saw Nic had left her some supper in the kitchen but she didn't feel like eating. Having a glass of water, she spent a moment with a drowsy Wallace and then climbed the stairs to her bedroom and had a quick shower. Wrapped in a soft, fluffy towel, she hesitated before walking along the corridor to Nic's room, feeling quite shameless as she slid into his bed.

For a few moments she watched him as he slept, sprawled on his front, face turned towards her on the pillow. Her heart swelled with a mixture of love and despair. Slowly, her fingers trailed across his shoulders and down his bare back and he stirred, sighing as he instinctively reached for her.

'Hannah…' he murmured, his dark eyes opening, lazy and slumberous.

Drawing her close, his mouth found hers, his hands roaming to all the places that made her tremble and whimper with desire as he made love to her with exquisite tenderness. When he finally fell asleep again, Hannah wiped at the tears that trickled down her cheeks, knowing she didn't have much longer with him.

* * *

Edgy and unsettled, Nic finished a new mother and baby clinic with Morag then went in search of Hannah, finding her in her consulting room writing up her notes.

'Hi,' she greeted him, wedging the files back into the tray and searching through a pile of papers on her desk. 'I meant to ask you for a second opinion on a patient. Where is the wretched thing?'

'Hannah, I—'

'Just a second. Ah, here it is! Can you take a look?'

Sighing, Nic took the papers she held out to him. 'Sure. Hannah, I need to ask you something.'

'Oh.' He saw her swallow, her green eyes clouding. 'Of course. What is it?'

'I'm going to need a few days away,' he explained.

'OK. Is this to do with your next job?' she asked, and he could gauge nothing from her tone.

'Yes.'

'Right.'

Nic wished she wouldn't hide her emotions. She gave nothing away and he had no idea what she wanted, how she felt about them, if this was just a pleasant interlude for her. She had never once asked if he would stay, had made no secret about making plans for his successor, as if his rapidly approaching departure meant little to her. Wouldn't she be at all sorry? As he tried to search her gaze now, she looked away, shuffling through her papers.

'Hannah—'

'Let me know when you want a reference or anything.'

Disgruntled, he gave up. 'Thanks. I'll read up about your patient and get back to you.'

'Fine.'

He left two days later, his heart heavy, hating Hannah's apparent acceptance but so confused in his own head he hadn't been able to talk to her about things. Them. The future. He needed this space away. His past made him wary of putting down roots again. Even more wary of caring too much, because everyone he loved had been taken from him and he couldn't go through that loss again. But he already cared for Hannah. More than cared. He'd been drawn to her from the first moment when she had been so prickly and scared, an intriguing mix of warmth and reserve, compassion and coolness, experience and innocence. Her aloneness had intrigued him, her pain had affected him, but finding the real Hannah underneath her defences had been the most joyous experience of his life. Having faced her fears, she had blossomed so beautifully, been so heart-stoppingly responsive, but she remained determinedly independent. While embracing their time together, she had asked for nothing, refused to discuss anything personal, given no indication of her feelings.

He ran a hand through his hair, confused and troubled. Don't stay in one place too long. Don't get involved. Those had been the maxims he had lived by these last two and more years, always on the move, always travelling light, unable to commit, unable to risk his heart again. Now he had broken all his rules. Sitting by the graves of his lost family and fiancée, he acknowledged that the thought of leaving Hannah for good was more painful than he could ever have expected. He'd helped her exorcise her ghosts, but what about his own? He closed his eyes, tipping his face to the warm Italian sun, his throat tight with emotion. What was he going to do?

The days Nic was away were the longest and most miserable Hannah had ever known. The house was empty and lonely without him. Even Wallace's company failed to lift her spirits, and she realised this was just a sample of what things would be like when he left for good. She slept in Nic's bed, cuddling his pillow, breathing in the lingering scent of him, her thoughts torturing her. Where in the world he would go next? Which place would know his healing touch? Which woman? The thought made her feel sick and brought a searing pain inside her. She missed him so much. Missed working with him and spending time with him at home. Missed his humour, his compassion. Missed sunny days off, exploring the southern uplands on his motorbike. Missed making love with him. No way could she ever let any other man touch her, not after Nic. She would be back in the old prison, but for a different reason.

Even the surgery was subdued, Kirsty prowling round like a grumpy lioness. 'Nic's gone for an interview?'

'I imagine so.'

Kirsty glared at her. 'You're just going to let him leave?'

'Nic has his own reasons for moving on. There's nothing I can do about that.' Hannah struggled to maintain her composure, fighting away the tears which seemed ever present. 'We knew he was only here for six months, that was the agreement. Now we have to find a permanent replacement.'

'I'm sorry, Hannah, but for such an intelligent woman you can be incredibly stupid sometimes. That man is the best thing that's happened to this place in years…and to you. We need him. You need him.'

'Kirsty—'

'If you seriously think no one knows what's going on between you, then you're even sillier than I thought,' the older woman lectured without mercy. 'It's been obvious from the first moment you were made for each other. I mean it, Hannah, you'll be all kinds of fool if you let Nic go.'

Hannah drew in a ragged breath as Kirsty turned on her heel and stomped out, closing the door none too quietly behind her. Of course she didn't want Nic to go. She loved him, for goodness' sake. But it wasn't in her power to stop him. He wasn't hers to keep. He'd made it plain from the beginning that he never stayed in one place, had never pretended anything else. And even if things had been different, she wasn't right for him. He deserved someone who could give him the family he craved. No matter what it cost her, she was not going to beg. She would not spoil the last special days they had together. Then she had to set him free. Free to find some other woman who could fulfil his needs. She closed her eyes against the unbearable pain.

Tired and unhappy, and with the out-of-hours

calls covered on the rota, Hannah went to bed early, taking Wallace up to Nic's room with her for company. She'd been alone before, had often chosen solitude, but she had never known this gut-wrenching, devastating emptiness. She tensed, hearing sounds in the house, her breath catching when she heard Nic's footsteps on the stairs and coming along the landing.

Colour washed her face as he came into the room, smiling when he saw her in his bed. 'Hi.'

'Hi.' She smiled back, voice husky. 'I had no idea you were coming back tonight.'

'I got a last-minute flight.'

He didn't question her presence there, rather than being in her own room while he was away. Instead, he dropped his overnight bag on the floor and shrugged out of his leather jacket.

'Did your trip go well?' She forced the question, dreading his reply. 'Have your sorted out your next move?'

'There are a couple of loose ends to tie up, but my plans are made.'

Disappointment and a burning sense of loss made her want to curl into a ball and cry. She was aware of a new calmness in him. Did that mean he was pleased to be leaving? 'That's good,' she murmured, her voice hoarse with reined-in emotion and bitter regret.

'I hate to deprive the little man, but I think Wallace would be better off downstairs.' Crossing to the bed, Nic scooped the sleepy kitten up in his arms. 'Hello, *uomo piccolo*, did you miss me?'

Hannah heard him chatting to Wallace as he left the room and she used the few moments alone to try and get her emotions back in check. She sucked in a ragged breath, overwhelmed Nic was home...for now. A frisson of excitement rippled through her at the thought of him being back in bed, making love with her. She had to extract every last second of pleasure she could to sustain her in the dark and dismal days that lay ahead when he left. When Nic arrived back in the bedroom, her pulse started to race. He looked rumpled and roguish, his dark hair mussed, a day or two's shadow of stubble darkening his jaw.

'I'm sorry,' she murmured, unsure how he felt about her sleeping there.

He paused in the process of taking off his boots and looked at her, one eyebrow raised in puzzlement. 'Excuse me?'

'For being in your bed. I wasn't expecting...' Her words trailed off at the heated, sultry expression in his eyes.

'Hannah, I wouldn't have wanted to find you anywhere else.'

His husky admission set awareness curling inside her. She watched, desire burning, as he slowly started to undress. Dear God, he was beautiful. Her fingers itched to touch him, her body tingling with the expectation of feeling him close again. Unselfconscious of his nakedness, he ran a hand across his jaw, glancing at her with a rueful smile.

'I'll go and shave.'

'Don't.' She flushed when he turned back, her voice a whisper. 'I like it.'

Eyes darkening, he walked towards the bed. Heart hammering under her ribs, Hannah slid over to make room for him, a sigh escaping when she felt the touch of his hands as he knelt over her.

'I think we should lose the pyjamas, cute as they are,' he decided, his fingers unbuttoning her top with tormenting slowness before he tossed it aside and turned his attention to the bottoms.

She trembled as he undressed her, desperate to have his mouth on her, eager to touch him, to taste him. 'Please, Nic.'

'All in good time, *amata*.'

He teased her, making her wait for the touches she craved until she thought she would explode with wanting. Impatient, her hands sank in the thickness of his hair, urging his head down, her lips parting in welcome, meeting the invasion of his tongue. His mouth moved on, working slowly down her neck, before worshipping first one breast, then the other, the rasp of his stubbled jaw on her skin an exciting caress. Breathless and needy, her hands conducted their own exploration, loving the smooth suppleness of skin over muscle, the perfection of his body that, for now, was hers to enjoy, to love. She gave everything she had to show him, without words, what he meant to her.

On Monday, with Nic taking extra patients, Hannah conducted a condensed early surgery and then began the preliminary interviews for the short-listed candidates who had applied for the permanent post of doctor at Lochanrig. Her heart wasn't in it. All she could think of was how perfect Nic was, not just as a friend and a lover but as a doctor. However well qualified, none of the people coming to see her would hold a candle to him, she just knew it.

The day was as long and unsatisfactory as she had anticipated. The assorted doctors had been qualified, but there was no sense of anticipation to work alongside any of them. A couple were over-confident, one quite the opposite, and one brash young man had been written off in the first five seconds by flirting brazenly with her. A frighteningly intense and earnest woman, well qualified on paper, was concerned about the rural location and whether her husband would find suitable employment locally. The only vague possibility was a married man looking to move with his wife and two children, but he was adamant he would not do out-of-hours work.

'Thank God that's over,' she grumbled when Kirsty stuck her head round the door.

'You have one more.'

Frowning, Hannah checked her appointment book and shook her head. 'Not listed here I haven't.'

'Sorry. Must be a clerical error,' Kirsty apologised, a strange expression twinkling in her eyes.

'Send them in, then, and let's get finished. I can't stand much more of this,' Hannah sighed, knowing this one would be as inappropriate as all the rest.

Frowning, she began searching through the papers on her desk for the extra CV and application form, glancing up as Nic sauntered in and closed the door. Her heart clenched painfully at the sight of him. Since he had come back from arranging his next contract, their love-making had been even more mind-blowing than before. She, who had thought she would never love anyone, who had been terrified of sex and intimacy, had fallen in love with Nic, had given him all of herself despite the knowledge he would walk out of her life all too soon. He, too, seemed different, the calmness she had noticed on his return bringing a new warmth and intensity to his every look and touch.

She tried to school her features into a mask of cool unconcern, banishing her body's traitorous response to him. 'Did you want something? Only I have another interview in a moment. Kirsty is just sending them in and I can't find the bloody form.'

'I know.' Nic smiled and sat down.

'Nic?'

'I'm waiting.'

Hannah frowned, in no mood for this. 'Waiting for what?

'For you to interview me.'

'Don't be silly.' Her heart lurched in disbelief. Tears stung her eyes. 'Nic, if this is some kind of joke, I don't find it remotely funny.'

'You refuse to consider my application? You don't want me here?'

He looked uncharacteristically nervous and uncertain, and his vulnerability was nearly her undoing. 'You w-want to stay?'

'I can't leave Wallace,' he stated, amusement shining in his eyes.

She wanted to scream with frustration. 'Nic, be serious.'

'Hannah, I've never been more serious about anything in my life,' he said, his voice rough, his sincerity tightening her chest and bringing a lump to her throat.

'Y-you said you wouldn't p-put down roots or do commitment again.'

'I was wrong. I met you.' Dark eyes filled with hope and something she didn't dare interpret. 'You said you could never love anyone.'

Hannah swallowed. She had said that. But then she hadn't known how magical loving Nic could be. 'I was wrong. I met you,' she whispered back.

He rose gracefully and came round the desk, taking her hands in his and drawing her to her feet. 'I love you, Hannah. I can no more leave you now than I can stop breathing. I love this place, these people. I've put down the deepest of roots these last months and I never want to leave. It's time for us both to step back into life—together. Will you have me? Will you let me buy into the practice and be your partner in all ways…in the surgery and in your life?'

Somehow she forced out the words. 'I can't, Nic.'

'Why not?' He looked pale with shock, eyes full of pain. 'Hannah, please.'

'It wouldn't be fair to you.'

He frowned, his hands tightening on hers. 'What are you talking about?'

'I'm not right for you. You want a family. I c-can't give you children, I—'

Tears squeezed between her lashes and he brushed them away with the pads of his thumbs before cupping her face in his hands. 'You don't know that for sure. But anyway, I want you, *amata*. There will be other Wallaces, other lives that need us, whatever happens. I need *you*. You are my family. All the people here in Lochanrig are my family.'

'You went away for another job,' she murmured, unable to believe this was really happening.

Nic shook his head. 'Not for another job. I went to Italy. It would have been Mama's birthday. I needed to get my head together, to exorcise my own ghosts and to say goodbye to the past before I could come back here, to you, for the present and the future.'

'I didn't know how you felt.'

'You think I could make love with you, the way we do, if I didn't feel anything?' he teased.

Hannah shrugged, a flush warming her face. 'I

don't know. I've not exactly had a lot of experience in that department, have I?'

'But you are a delightfully quick learner!' Nic's dark eyes twinkled naughtily. 'And you can have all the practice you want—but only with me.' His expression sobered. 'I had no idea how you felt, either, if what we had meant anything to you. You gave nothing away, just planned for the day I would be gone. So I took a chance. I had to. I can't lose you. What do you say, Hannah? Please, will you marry me and let me love you for the rest of our lives?'

'Yes! Oh, yes, Nic! I love you so much.'

His kiss took her breath away. She wound her arms round him, pressing herself against him, giving thanks for the day this caring, sexy man had bulldozed his way into her life.

This special doctor with his healing touch had given her new hope and a rich new life filled with a love and a passion she had never expected to know.

MEDICAL ROMANCE™

Large Print

Titles for the next six months…

May

THE CHRISTMAS MARRIAGE RESCUE Sarah Morgan
THEIR CHRISTMAS DREAM COME TRUE   Kate Hardy
A MOTHER IN THE MAKING   Emily Forbes
THE DOCTOR'S CHRISTMAS PROPOSAL   Laura Iding
HER MIRACLE BABY   Fiona Lowe
THE DOCTOR'S LONGED-FOR BRIDE Judy Campbell

June

THE MIDWIFE'S CHRISTMAS MIRACLE Sarah Morgan
ONE NIGHT TO WED   Alison Roberts
A VERY SPECIAL PROPOSAL   Josie Metcalfe
THE SURGEON'S MEANT-TO-BE BRIDE Amy Andrews
A FATHER BY CHRISTMAS   Meredith Webber
A MOTHER FOR HIS BABY   Leah Martyn

July

THE SURGEON'S MIRACLE BABY   Carol Marinelli
A CONSULTANT CLAIMS HIS BRIDE   Maggie Kingsley
THE WOMAN HE'S BEEN WAITING FOR
                                        Jennifer Taylor
THE VILLAGE DOCTOR'S MARRIAGE Abigail Gordon
IN HER BOSS'S SPECIAL CARE   Melanie Milburne
THE SURGEON'S COURAGEOUS BRIDE   Lucy Clark

MILLS & BOON®

0407 LP 2P P1 Medica

MEDICAL ROMANCE™

—⋀— *Large Print* —⋀—

August

A WIFE AND CHILD TO CHERISH   Caroline Anderson
THE SURGEON'S FAMILY MIRACLE   Marion Lennox
A FAMILY TO COME HOME TO   Josie Metcalfe
THE LONDON CONSULTANT'S RESCUE   Joanna Neil
THE DOCTOR'S BABY SURPRISE   Gill Sanderson
THE SPANISH DOCTOR'S CONVENIENT BRIDE
                                     Meredith Webber

September

A FATHER BEYOND COMPARE   Alison Roberts
AN UNEXPECTED PROPOSAL   Amy Andrews
SHEIKH SURGEON, SURPRISE BRIDE   Josie Metcalfe
THE SURGEON'S CHOSEN WIFE   Fiona Lowe
A DOCTOR WORTH WAITING FOR Margaret McDonagh
HER L.A. KNIGHT   Lynne Marshall

October

HIS VERY OWN WIFE AND CHILD   Caroline Anderson
THE CONSULTANT'S NEW-FOUND FAMILY Kate Hardy
CITY DOCTOR, COUNTRY BRIDE   Abigail Gordon
THE EMERGENCY DOCTOR'S DAUGHTER   Lucy Clark
A CHILD TO CARE FOR   Dianne Drake
HIS PREGNANT NURSE   Laura Iding

MILLS & BOON®

0407 LP 2P P2 Medical